KARMA

KARMA

The Force of Justice

A Fantasy Romance

Carolyn van Dijk

KARMA
THE FORCE OF JUSTICE

iUniverse books may be ordered through booksellers or by contacting:

iUniverse
1663 Liberty Drive
Bloomington, IN 47403
www.iuniverse.com
1-800-Authors (1-800-288-4677)

Because of the dynamic nature of the Internet, any web addresses or links contained in this book may have changed since publication and may no longer be valid. The views expressed in this work are solely those of the author and do not necessarily reflect the views of the publisher, and the publisher hereby disclaims any responsibility for them.

Any people depicted in stock imagery provided by Thinkstock are models, and such images are being used for illustrative purposes only. Certain stock imagery © Thinkstock.

ISBN: 978-1-4917-6368-1 (sc)
ISBN: 978-1-4917-6367-4 (e)
Library of Congress Control Number: 2015905286

Print information available on the last page.

iUniverse rev. date: 04/20/2015

Acknowledgements

This book was written for pleasure, but it also makes a point. Although I do not actually believe in reincarnation or karma, I do believe in fairness and justice. I want to thank all those who helped in the making of my first novel. This book perhaps displays a fantasy of mine.

Some of the characters are based on real people, but not entirely, and I in no way mean to offend anyone. Names have been changed to protect the innocent (and the not so innocent).

Carolyn

To my four sons,
David, Daniel, Mark and Michael,
my legacies.

Carmen Hamilton sat in the dark, a half-moon above her, a few clouds occasionally crossing in front of it and leaving the cool night even darker. Below her shone the lights of the little town. She could see her cozy old house from where she sat, only a block from downtown. In the other direction, she could see the hospital where she worked as a nurse.

She sat watching over her town beside the ugliest gargoyle, which she had named Ralph. He reminded her of her Grade 1 teacher: ugly, mean and jealous of her intelligence. She gathered then that she was different. She had been tempted a couple times to use her ability to get back at Mr. Butler, but she had been raised with good ethics and had vowed as she matured to her present age of thirty-five that she would only use her gift for good.

However, even though Ralph reminded her of a person that she did not have fond memories of, she liked him and sat beside him most times when she wanted to oversee her fellow citizens living their lives.

She thought back to the first time she comprehended having special powers. She was just a small child, and her mother had told her that she couldn't have a cookie before supper. She became angry and flipped a dish off the table. Her mother of course thought that she had used her hands, but she had done it with her mind.

She didn't think this was unusual until she noticed that other people did not do it, and later she came to realize that her ability scared people when they saw it. At first her mother, Norma, punished her for it, but when Carmen got back at her with a ripped dress or an overturned vase, this frightened her mother. Carmen did realize eventually that this was not the thing to do to someone she loved, and she learned how to control her emotions and actions.

She tried to respect her mother, but by her teens, she felt like her mother treated her unfairly. Her sister, Jill, who had no strange powers, was certainly the favourite, but Carmen loved Jill and never resented her for that.

Carmen's father did not stick up for her; he seemed not to care about much at all. He was distant and spent a lot of time out of the house. He ultimately walked out on the family.

Norma became more controlling after Carmen's father left and limited all Carmen's activities. She was not pleasant at all, and Carmen was happy to leave for university. She had distanced herself from her mother since then.

Well, I had better go home and go to bed, Carmen thought. She floated down slowly into an alley beside the old bank Ralph the gargoyle adorned, where no one was likely to see her using her power of levitation. She was tall and slender with long, dark, silky hair; big brown eyes with long, dark lashes; and sculpted cheekbones on a friendly face. She stood out enough without showing her skill.

Back on the street, she saw a man kick a poor stray dog rummaging for something to eat. It angered her how cruel some people could be. The puddle on the side of the street seemed to give her a perfect opportunity: She willed a large truck to veer just close enough to the curb to splash water over the dog-kicking man. A tinge of guilt came over her as the man shook the water from his coat. *Oh well. At least I didn't have the truck hit him. As they say, "What goes around comes around."*

Carmen woke to another rainy day. The clouds were dark and heavy. *On the bright side*, she thought, *at least there will be more puddles if I need one.* She giggled.

The air was fresh and the temperature was mild, just the way she liked it. *I don't know why I was disappointed to see rain today. It is renewing*, she thought.

The dripping of the falling rain sounded like elves playing tiny instruments, and wind chimes tinkled at some of her neighbours' houses.

The birds loved the rain. Seeing them bathe in the puddles reminded Carmen that her birdbath would be overflowing today.

On her walk to work, she remembered the first time that she understood that her powers could be quite useful. All she had to do was will something, and it came about. She didn't have to do the action physically; she could mentally manipulate objects and bodies.

She had healed a cat that had been hit by a car just by wishing for it. She had cured her grandmother's cancer, too. Her grandmother had known about Carmen's ability and encouraged the healing. Carmen had promised her that she would only use it for good, so she justified some of the cruel things she did by reminding herself that she was penalizing the recipient for his or her offence.

Carmen had stopped car accidents and stopped people from falling, but she had also caused people to fall. She had once made a rapist impotent. She changed streetlights, caused lightning and summoned insects. She would not sway sports events, though, because they had no link to justice. She had locked a cheating husband in his car for an hour when he went to meet his mistress, but he still went to see the home wrecker when Carmen had freed him. So then she locked him out of his car.

When she neared the hospital, she remembered the elderly man she had met the day before. He had touched her with his positive attitude. He didn't have much longer to live, but he was so grateful for the life he *had* lived, the life he had been blessed with, as he had put it. It had not always been an easy life. His father had died when he was young, and he had lost a child when he was grown. However, he had always lived his life the way Carmen wished everyone would live: always giving back to society, not taking with an angry heart. And his wife was lovely. Oh, how Carmen yearned to have a love like theirs.

The wind pulling at her wet umbrella brought Carmen back to the present. As she waited for the Walk sign at the crosswalk, she watched a well-dressed woman turn her nose up at a disheveled man asking for loose change. Her hope was restored when a young university student dropped some coins in his hand. *Hmmm, how can I reward this young pupil?* she thought. It would not take him long to notice the twenty-dollar bill she telepathically stuck to the bottom of his shoe.

The light changed, and the crowd crossed the street like a school of fish, smoothly, in unison, all of them with purpose.

Carmen reached Oakland District Hospital, where she had worked as a nurse for years. This was the only hospital in the town of Oakland, Ontario, a busy town full of mature trees and parks with a small river running through it to the lake. Carmen had been born and raised in this town and enjoyed giving back to the community that she loved.

As she walked through the automatic sliding glass doors, she took a deep breath, lifted her head high and put herself into her professional role.

The building had been recently renovated with the generous donation of a powerful individual in the community. At least that was what everyone thought of him. Carmen had arranged for one of the kingpins in town to "lose" a little money from one of his offshore accounts.

The walls in the lobby were freshly painted in a soft lavender, and new furniture, artwork and equipment embellished every department.

She reached her department on one of the medical floors, this one painted a soft sage green to distinguish it from the other floors with identical layouts. The fluorescent lighting showed every flaw in the old structure, especially where changes such as moved walls and doorways had been made over the many years that the hospital had been in existence.

She greeted her coworkers every day, paying special attention to the handsome thirty-six-year-old gentle biomedical engineer, Peter Anderson. He made her heart skip a beat with his brown curly hair, dark soft eyes, and a body typical of a man with a physical job. He was about six foot two and one hundred eighty pounds, well-toned, and groomed to a tee. He even looked good in the blue workman uniform he was forced to wear. However, he was a guy who acted as if he didn't know he was good-looking.

Their eyes met, he smiled, she melted and her knees went weak.

"Good morning, Carmen," he said. "Hey, the Howling Dogs' new album is out."

"Yes, I've got to get it. Have you got it yet?"

"Not yet, but, ummm ..." He hesitated. "How about hitting the music store together? Tonight, maybe?"

Carmen couldn't remember him seeming so unsure of himself before. Was he asking her out? Was it a good idea to date someone from work? Oh, but how she wanted to. She wanted someone in her life again. It had been so long. Moreover, she wanted Peter.

She had not been lucky in love at all. It seemed that all the men that she liked weren't interested in her, but the ones that she wasn't interested in came out of the woodwork. She had never openly shown her powers to any boyfriends, but sometimes things happened that scared them off. Since school, Carmen had been known as the person around whom strange things occurred.

She had liked Peter for a long time now. They were friends; she knew that. She knew what kind of person he was. Oh, to be held by those arms! Had she been daydreaming? *Oh my. For how long?* she wondered.

"Yes … sure," she stammered almost as shyly as he had sounded. *This is okay, isn't it? After all, it's only a shopping trip, not really a date.*

During her shift, she daydreamed about going to the store with Peter. She also manipulated things a few times to recompense the deserving and punish the offenders. Having a passion for justice and a sensitive heart, and supernatural skills, she tasked herself with bringing people their dues.

Carmen cursed Betty Chase, a veteran nurse who was losing her compassion and gaining contempt, with a rash that would increase in size with every bitter word she inflicted on fellow staff, student nurses and patients that day. This was a little justice given by an extraordinary prosecutor in a nurse's uniform.

The trip to the music store turned out to be a pleasant excursion. Peter made her laugh. She felt so at ease with him. She could totally be herself. As he talked, Carmen found herself staring at his teeth, of all things. Like perfect Chiclets—okay, not that big. Corn lined up on a cob— okay, no, certainly not like yellow corn. They had no comparison; they were just perfect teeth on the gorgeous face of a genuine man.

They each bought the CD of the band they both loved. Carmen had discovered them about a year before when she had asked what he was listening to on his Mp3 player.

After the music store, they grabbed a coffee at the shop next door and talked for a while. Peter then walked her to her car, kissed her on the cheek, and said, "see you tomorrow."

What was that? she thought on her way home. *Is he playing hard to get, or does he just want to be friends? Well, I guess it didn't help that I insisted we drive there in our own cars.* She was so preoccupied that she didn't even remember the drive when she got home.

Planning to skip her people-watching from the roof of the bank tonight, she curled up with a cup of Earl Grey tea for a game of solitaire on her tablet. Cozy under her blanket, she attempted not to overthink the evening with Peter.

She turned on the TV to watch the news before retiring for the night. The news inspired her to imagine giving nasty people a taste of their own medicine. Tonight, one of the highlights was about a missing child, Brandon Harrison, only seven years old. He had last been seen playing in his family's front yard. When he didn't answer his mother's call, she began to call neighbours. One had seen a green minivan drive by numerous times right after lunch. By dinner time, no one had seen him, and his parents frantically called the police.

This story made Carmen feel sick. *Those poor parents,* she thought. But all she needed was the description of the minivan to do her thing. She willed its owner to drive into a lamp post, but not hard enough to hurt any passengers.

At the nurses' station the next day, the hustle and bustle had begun. Night nurses with faces betraying their tired bodies reached for their bags and wished the day staff a good shift.

"Carmen, you forgot to sign this yesterday!" Tina Moretti roared as she held up a patient's chart.

Tina wasn't as bad as Betty, but she did like to accuse people of making mistakes. *She must be terribly insecure,* Carmen guessed. She looked at the chart. "I wasn't supposed to sign it. It's not even my patient."

"Well *someone* forgot to sign it," Tina grumbled, turning to the other nurses.

Carmen imagined a hand with one finger pointing and three others pointing back at the accuser. She left Tina with a fat, red pimple on her nose.

Just in time to change the mood, Mrs. Hofstadter came along, smiling her toothless smile as she pushed her IV pole. "Nurse, may I go sit in the lounge?" she asked Carmen.

"Sure, and I will come and bring you your lunch when it arrives."

"Why don't you tell her to stay in her room for lunch?" Tina demanded. "We aren't waitresses, you know. And if you let her have her lunch delivered, then they'll all want it."

"Do to others as you would have them do to you," Carmen recited.

"Pfff." Tina turned away.

My, that pimple looks angry. Carmen laughed inwardly as she turned away from Tina. She knew the testy woman's pimple would sprout in full glory as the day went on, and that satisfied her. The woman deserved it. Perhaps a pimple was too mild a sentence, but there was always another day.

Peter came to Carmen's department to see if she had a chance to listen to the CD. Of course she had, and had thought of him while listening, but she would never tell him that.

"Can you get away for lunch at around noon?" he asked.

"I'll try. Sometimes it just doesn't work out to meet at an exact time," Carmen admitted.

"I understand." Peter knew how it was.

The hours passed, and soon it was time for lunch. Carmen brought Mrs. Hofstadter's lunch to her in the lounge when it came up from the kitchen. Mrs. Hofstadter was so pleased with the little extra service and kindness that Carmen offered. Her smile brought warmth to Carmen's heart, almost making her feel guilty for receiving the benefit from her act. That was certainly not why she did it. She did it to bring joy to a patient who had to stay in the hospital instead of being at home.

Carmen continued on to make sure that her other patients all got their lunches, and she gave them their medications, enjoying every bit of chitchat that came with her job.

Peter came by at noon and waited for her. She didn't take too long. Then they took the elevator downstairs together and sat on a bench in the sun at the side of the hospital.

"I had a great time last night," Peter said. "Would you grace me with your presence again?"

She chuckled at his attempt at old-fashioned charm, and he pulled a face as if sickened by his own pretentiousness. "I would love to." She contemplated whether she should have stalled by saying she had to check her calendar first. *Oh, heck. Just forget it. You know you have nothing going on. Just be honest with the guy.* Carmen hated playing games. *If I like the guy, why not give him a clue?*

"Can I pick you up at home later and take you out for dinner? We could go for a walk after we eat, if it isn't too cold out."

"That would be very nice," she said as she looked into his eyes. With the sun shining directly on her, she could see her reflection. She liked it; it meant that she was close to him.

"I'll text you later then, okay?" Peter said. "I have to get back to work."

"Okay."

Time dragged as Carmen looked forward to their date. When it was finally the end of her shift, she practically ran out the door.

She had to watch how fast she drove home, and occasionally the speedometer indicated that she would have gotten a ticket had police been in view. When she reached her house, she left the car on the driveway and hurried inside.

A little later she received a text saying that he would be there around four thirty, if that was okay with her. She texted back, "Sure, that would be great." She dressed in a lilac-coloured dress cut just above the knee and with a round neckline showing off her amethyst necklace. She donned pale grey pumps with a slender heel.

Peter arrived promptly at four thirty. He was out of his heavy blue uniform and wearing jeans, a grey-and-white striped golf shirt and a black leather jacket. His hair looked as if it was still wet. He drove a classic Chevelle in lime green with a black stripe down the hood. *It suits him,* Carmen thought. She remembered seeing it in the parking lot and commenting to him about it before. The car was immaculate, just like he was.

"You must have a beater for the winter so this one sits pampered in the garage, right?" she said more than asked.

"I have a pickup truck, too," Peter assured her. He opened the car door for her. "I'm impressed that you know what kind of car this is."

"I know most cars from that era. That was when guys drove muscle cars, not the stupid pimpmobiles the boys drive nowadays."

Peter laughed. "That's for sure."

They hadn't learned a whole lot about each other in the years they had both worked at the hospital. They usually engaged in small talk when they spoke. During the drive, they elaborated on their love of the Howling Dogs, and Carmen learned that he liked nature. "I have a Sheltie named Shelley and a cat named Oscar. And he isn't a grouch. He is a real cuddler." He laughed.

Carmen listened intently and told him that she loved animals too. "I feed the animals in my yard, and I had pets growing up, but none now. I don't want to leave them home alone while I'm at work.

"I agree. That's why I don't just have one pet." Peter put the car in Park.

He came around and opened the car door for Carmen again and led her to the restaurant, Bella Italia, saying he figured Italian food would be a safe choice. His mother had told him to plan dates and not to run by the seat of his pants. "Don't ever ask your date, 'So what do you want to do?' she told me."

He seemed very fond of his mother. Carmen looked up at the sign. "I've never been here before."

"That's good, we'll start our own memories." He took her hand.

When they entered, Carmen had to stop to take it all in. The walls were made of brick with weeping-mortar joints, like an old European building. The ceiling contained large wooden beams with ivy laced across them and running down the walls and archways, which were also made of brick. Little tables with blue gingham tablecloths and candles in the centre stood in rows. Clusters of red garlic hung in the windows with wrought-iron muntins. Palms stood in the corners, and the far wall was covered with a floor-to-ceiling wine rack of dark wood filled with bottles of every variety of wine imaginable.

"This is beautiful, Peter. How cozy."

"I'm glad you like it. I haven't been here before either, so I wasn't sure what to expect. But it came highly recommended."

"Table for two?" the hostess asked.

"Yes, please." Peter waited as Carmen went first and followed her.

The hostess sat them in a quiet corner by a window. Peter thanked her.

"This should keep the vampires away," Carmen said, pointing to a garlic cluster.

"Oh, darn, I was hoping to do a little chewing on your neck later."

"Oh, no! Are you a vampire?" Carmen said with exaggerated drama.

"I might be some kind of voracious creature, but I'll stick to pasta tonight. What about you? What kind of creature would you be?"

Carmen started, almost spilling her glass of water. "What?" She swallowed hard.

"If you could be a mythical creature, what would you be? A vampire, werewolf, a witch?"

"Yeah, a witch," she answered. *If you only knew.*

"A good witch or an ugly green one with a wart on her big pointy nose?"

"I'm not so sure what kind I would be. It depends on your point of view."

"What?" Peter looked puzzled. "Well, from my point of view, you would be a beautiful good witch."

I sure hope so, Carmen thought.

Peter ordered chicken cacciatore, and Carmen ordered chicken parmesan. They began their meal with the bottomless Caesar salad.

"This is so nice, Peter," Carmen said gratefully. "I'm glad you invited me. Thank you."

"You're very welcome. It is all my pleasure," Peter answered nobly. "Their spaghetti is supposed to be really good here, but I can make that at home myself, so I tried something else."

Carmen saw the perfect opportunity to play with Peter and caused the cheese to stretch from his mouth as he put the spoon back on the plate. With a look of distaste, he pulled the cheese off his lip and wiped his mouth with his napkin.

Maybe I had better keep my skills under wraps a bit longer, she decided. He had been easily perturbed by the threat to his manners.

"Would you like to go to the pond nearby after dinner to see the swans?" Peter asked.

"I'd like that."

They passed on dessert. Peter paid the bill and then helped Carmen with her chair. Her shoes clicked on the terra cotta floor.

As they headed toward a bench by the pond, Peter reached for her hand and held it while they walked. Carmen felt butterflies in her stomach being beside him. She could smell his cologne and found herself even more attracted to him than she had at dinner. He had such impeccable manners, pulling out the chair for her, asking what she wanted, and ordering for her. How gallant he was.

He seemed to be everything she had dreamed of in a man. She hoped she wasn't setting herself up for heartbreak or disappointment.

Children came nearby to see the swans, laughing and

playing. Peter and Carmen laughed at their antics and the novelty they experienced with the swans.

"I love the little cygnets," Carmen said.

"Show-off. I like the baby swans too," Peter teased.

Carmen telepathically called the carp to come to the shore, and the children were mesmerized by the fish's gaping mouths.

Peter smiled at Carmen and put his arm around her, pulling her close beside him on the bench. Another whiff of his cologne tingled her nostrils.

"I like kids," he said. "They have such a great outlook."

"Me too. Do you want to have any?" Carmen probed hopefully.

"Sure. Right here, right now." He waggled his eyebrows and nudged her sideways onto the bench and almost lay on top of her.

"I meant do you plan to have any?" She laughed and straightened herself.

He helped her sit upright. "I want some one day, before I get too old."

She was relieved because she had always known that she wanted to be a mother. It was no use getting involved with a man who didn't want to have children too.

After about an hour, the air grew cooler, so Peter took her to a coffee shop. He ordered coffee for each of them and carried both mugs to the table.

"This is nicer than paper cups," Carmen said.

"That's for sure," Peter said. "Styrofoam is the worst."

"I've always said the same thing." She felt like they had a lot in common. *Let's see how he takes his coffee.*

He slid the cream and sugar dispensers toward Carmen, and she poured her double cream and two sugars. She smiled and slid them back to him.

He poured the same. "Double-double."

"Me too."

"I noticed. Not that you need all that sugar."

"I know it isn't good for me, but they make coffee so strong."

"Actually, I meant that you were sweet enough. Sorry, corny and cliché, I know." Peter looked down at his mug.

"Not corny; it's nice. I like to get compliments. I just don't handle them very well," Carmen admitted.

"Why not?" Peter asked.

"I guess I just never got enough of them. Maybe my mom was afraid to make me conceited." Carmen tried to laugh to diminish the pain.

"You are far from conceited, and you deserve the compliment. You *are* sweet. You are lovely, beautiful, smart, and ..." He paused. "Sexy."

"Thanks. You're sweet too, and handsome and smart, and ..." she whispered the last word: "sexy." Her face got hot. She had never told someone that by the second date before. However, she felt free to do so with Peter, especially since he had said it first. But she knew she couldn't tell him everything about herself yet.

They talked and laughed until 10:00 p.m., and then Peter asked, "Do you have to work tomorrow?"

"Yes," she said disappointedly. "You?"

"Yes," he said with disdain in his voice. "I had better drive you home. I'm sorry if I kept you too late.

"No, not at all." Carmen didn't want him to feel sorry, because she hadn't wanted to leave any sooner.

He led her to the car and opened the large, heavy door. She smoothed her dress and got inside.

"Did I tell you how beautiful you look?" Peter asked before he closed the door.

"You did."

"You look even more beautiful out of uniform. I mean, without your scrubs … I mean, oh shit, in that dress." He shut the door.

Carmen giggled. She wondered if she would get a kiss on the cheek again. She sure was hoping she'd get a full-blown smack on the lips this time. She imagined his lips on hers the whole way home.

At Carmen's house, Peter walked her to her door. The porch light was on, but the morning glories growing up the trellis sheltered them from spying eyes and the lights of downtown.

He lifted her chin with his finger and stared at her for what seemed like an eternity because she wanted so much for him to hurry and kiss her. Then it happened: the softest, warmest, sexiest kiss she had ever felt. His lips were full, and she felt his passion.

Carmen had fallen more in love with him in the last few days that they spent together than she had in all the years that she had known him at work. *Why did we wait so long?* she thought. *Fear.*

Oh, how she heated up in his arms. She pulled away slowly. *Not so fast*, she thought. *Don't rush; that might ruin it.*

She smiled up at him. Pulling his hands from her shoulders, she took one small step backwards. *Let him yearn for me.*

It was so hard to end the evening. "Thanks for such a great time," she managed to whisper with a sigh. He looked bewildered, injured. She didn't want to hurt him. "I don't want to rush," she added.

He nodded.

Oh good. He understands.

She winked at him. "See you at work." She turned to go in, aching inside.

She liked that he waited on the porch until she was safely inside her house. She smiled as she closed the door. She watched him walk down the path and granted him a cluster of fireflies to light his way back to his car. She watched him drive away. That night, she dreamed of him.

2

Waking after a night of pleasant dreams, Carmen readied herself for work, going through her usual routine but with an added bounce in her step. The birds came to her windowsill, where she left food for them every morning.

A squirrel then scared them all away. "Hey, you bully." She laughed. "The peanuts are in the backyard. This stuff isn't for you." The grey squirrel looked up at her through the window and sat up on his back legs as if to start a conversation. She opened the window, and the furry creature stayed. She spoke softly to him, but when she reached for him, he jumped into the huge old oak tree in Carmen's front yard and chattered at her. She laughed. Rushing to finish her morning preparations, she forgot the squirrel and the open window.

Downstairs, she noticed the kids from next door fighting outside. The older one was always picking on the smaller one. "You're stupid and I don't want to walk you to school!" he bellowed, making the little girl cry.

Carmen stepped onto her porch and locked the front door. On the bottom step, she said, "Steven, your mother depends on you to be a good big brother to Vanessa."

There was no calming him this morning. He stuck his tongue out at her, pushed his sister out of his way, and ran off to school. Vanessa ran to catch up, wiping tears from her face.

"Atta girl, Vanessa! Catch him!" Carmen called after her.

Carmen urged the blue jay flying overhead to drop a white bomb on the nasty little boy—splat! Right on his shoulder. "Eeewww!" he howled.

Carmen laughed. "Serves you right!" she said softly.

Carmen enjoyed the walk to work. She stopped for coffee on her way, planning to drink most of it before she reached the hospital. While she stood in line, the cashier complained that the patron she was serving was short a quarter for her order of coffee and a bagel. People in line sighed and grumbled, but only one person, a middle-aged man, offered to contribute the quarter himself.

It seemed that the patron had ordered all she could afford, and she thanked the man incessantly. He seemed embarrassed, as he was unable to make eye contact with the woman. However, he also seemed impatient, and Carmen guessed that he had only paid the quarter to speed up the line.

Well, no bonus for you today, Carmen thought. *I only reward those with a true generosity. And I could have given you a bottomless cup of coffee, too.*

Carmen continued her walk to work with fond recollections of Peter. She couldn't wait to see him today. Then, there he was waiting at the front door for her. She felt her stomach leap into her throat.

There was that smile again. He held the door for her and wished her a good morning. "I wasn't sure that you came in this door. I hope it isn't too bold of me to wait for you here. I just couldn't wait to see you. Maybe that was too audacious of me as well. I just think that if somebody likes someone, they should say so, and if you don't feel the same way, then just tell me to hit the road."

"Well, I certainly don't want you to hit the road," Carmen replied. "I like that you're here, and I have the same philosophy about being upfront with people." She accepted his outstretched hand and headed inside.

When they reached her floor, he asked, "May I kiss you before I say goodbye?"

"We might start a scandal, you know." She laughed. "You know how people talk about workplace relationships."

He laughed too. "Good. I love a good scandal, especially if I'm in it." He kissed her long and hard before leaving her at the elevator.

Carmen turned away from Peter and stopped short when she saw Diana Mason, another nurse, standing a few feet away grinning at her.

"Wow! What was that?" Diana said, her eyes wide. "It's about time!"

Carmen and Diana had been friends for a long time, and they worked well together. They had talked about Peter before.

Carmen just smiled, blushing, she was sure, as she headed to her locker.

"Tell me, tell me!" Diana begged, tugging on Carmen's sleeve. "When did this start?"

"Just a couple days ago," Carmen told her. "He invited me to the record store, and then yesterday we went out for dinner."

"Didn't I always tell you to go after him?" Diana reminded her.

"I know, but I wanted him to pursue me." Carmen closed her locker, and she and Diana commenced their assignments for the day.

That evening, dying for some time by herself after a noisy day, Carmen floated up to sit by Ralph. Still alone, although near so many people. It was quiet up here above the bank, quieter than at street level, for sure.

What would Peter think if he really knew about her? Should she even disclose such a thing? *Let's not worry about that right now*, she decided.

The moon was a little fuller tonight than the last time she had sat on the roof, and there were fewer clouds, so it was easier to see things going on below. A woman dropped a glove, and another woman picked it up and returned it. Carmen also noticed a man excuse himself for bumping into someone, a young man hold open a door for an old woman, and a store clerk carry a box to a customer's car. Carmen was pleased with all this kindness and acknowledged them with a gentle, warm breeze full of the fragrance of lilacs.

She basked in their responses to this delight, the

smiles, the lifted noses, the closed eyes. She imagined that she could hear their sighs.

Carmen then decided to pick up cupcakes to hand out at work the next day. She would enjoy her coworkers' finger licking and lip smacking. She loved that the cashier's jaw dropped when Carmen pointed out that she had given Carmen too much change. The cashier probably didn't hear that too often. People always mentioned when they were short-changed but not when they received too much.

At home, the mess Carmen found disconcerted her. Things had been strewn about, and the more valuable items were missing. How had this happened? Why? Who did it? *Damn it*, she thought. *I am always watching people for their misdeeds, and now a big one has happened right under my nose.*

She remembered her small box of heirloom jewellery her grandmother had given her. She ran quickly to her bedroom. "No!" she cried. The small pewter box was missing. She hunted; still no sign of it. Then she noticed the open window. *Oh, crap. The squirrel this morning. How could I have been so stupid as to leave the window wide open?*

The special gifts from her beloved grandmother, passed down to her just before she died, were irreplaceable memories of the woman she loved more than her own mother, of the woman who had always been there for her when her mother had turned away.

Carmen fell to her knees. Anger rose inside her. "Confound it!" she began. "I stand for goodness every day, and this is how I get rewarded?" She pounded her hands on her thighs. "Why bother?"

She rose, burst out the back door into the yard, and swiftly lofted to the gabled roof. "I'll get you, you bastard! I'll get you!"

What a sight that would have been for the neighbours, she mused after calming down a little. She ventured out into the night to look for any sign of the pilfering creeps that stole from her, and from her grandmother. She returned home after about an hour and then called the police.

Carmen didn't know it, but she had nearly caught the burglars when she silently came in the front door just as they were bundling their takings by the back door. So close!

It had been so easy to come in that open window and then let his partners in the door. Too bad they couldn't go back for more. That would be pressing their luck because the homeowner would be on her guard now.

The young man went through his loot and recognized that he hadn't gotten anything all that good. The electronics were always easy to sell, and his buddies had already taken the stuff they wanted to keep, but he and his accomplices hadn't been able to carry that much and run at the same time. The jewellery wasn't in style right now. It would be harder to get rid of. He would bring it to a pawnshop on the other side of town some time when he felt like it. Why did people even save this crap? Maybe it was just junk and he should trash it. Na, he had to get something out of it. He headed out to see what other trouble he could get into.

Carmen felt uncomfortable in her own home that night and had difficulty sleeping. She tossed; when she did finally manage to fall asleep, she woke with a start at every noise.

She took the next day off, telling her supervisor that her home had been burglarized. She knew she wouldn't be able to focus on her work. Now no one could partake in the cupcakes she had bought.

She dressed, combed her hair and got into her car. She grabbed a coffee at a drive-through and then ventured from pawnshop to pawnshop with pictures of her treasures, asking the clerks to notify her if anyone should come in with these things. Most of them were friendly but indifferent to Carmen's plight. She knew that they knew that most of the items in their stores were stolen property.

When she got home, she collapsed in her chair, just in time for Peter's phone call.

"I'm so sorry, Carmen," he said with sincere concern in his voice. "I just heard from coworkers what happened. It's horrible, but I'm so glad that you weren't hurt. You know, you could have come home while they were still there, and they could have killed you. I don't mean to scare you. I just want to say how relieved I am. Things can be replaced, but you cannot."

Carmen accepted his cliché and thanked him for calling.

He told her that he would be over right after work, considering how close she was to tears as she told him what happened. "I'll even try to get off work early."

Carmen managed a fitful nap on the couch while she waited for him. Getting up, she checked for the third time that she had locked the doors and windows.

Peter came over as he said he would and held her close to console her. "I'm sorry I couldn't get off earlier. I can stay with you if you'll feel safer that way."

"I'm so glad you came. I didn't want to bother my sister or get a lecture about forgetfulness from my mother. I spent the day running to crumby pawn shops to give them a heads-up. It probably won't do any good, though."

Peter poured a cup of herbal tea and handed it to Carmen. She cradled it in her hands, enjoying the warmth.

"Have you eaten anything today?" he asked.

"No."

Peter made some toast. The smell made Carmen feel a little more at home again, and his being here made her feel safe again. She no longer heard every creak, the ticking of the clock, or the hum of the fridge. "I know now what people mean when they say they feel violated. The idea of strangers going through my stuff makes my skin crawl. Even worse, they took my grandmother's things. Those heirlooms were special to me. My grandmother was my confidant, my go-to person, my mentor, my friend." She burst into tears. "I remember those pieces being on her wrists, neck, and fingers. Now who knows where they are!"

"Would it help if we looked at some photographs of your grandmother together?" Peter offered. "Do you have an album? Shall I get it?"

"On the bookshelf." Carmen pointed. She put her empty mug on the table, pulled her legs up, and folded them under herself.

Peter returned to the couch with the album that she had indicated. He sat beside her and handed her the large, heavy book.

She opened it on her lap. Photographs of a tiny baby wrapped in a blanket or in sleepers in a crib graced the first page.

"Is that you?" Peter guessed. "You have always been beautiful. Just look at that cute face."

Carmen smiled. She turned the page to photographs of her grandmother holding the baby.

"Now that is one proud grandma," Peter said.

Carmen beamed, but then her expression tightened. "This is my mom." She pointed to a picture of a younger woman holding that same baby. As they flipped through the book, Carmen grew, but her mother was in fewer pictures with her. Usually the mother was behind the camera, but not in this case. Carmen's grandmother or grandfather had taken most of these.

"You were a sweet little girl." Peter looked at her. "Now you're a sweet woman." He kissed her gently.

She laid her head on his shoulder, and he pulled her close.

"Is that your dad?" Peter asked, pointing to the first picture on the next page.

"Yes. I have only one picture of him. My mother destroyed the rest."

"Let me guess: angry, scorned woman, right?"

"Exactly. He left us, so she got rid of anything that reminded her of him. I managed to save this picture from her bonfire."

"I'm sorry, Carmen. You haven't had it easy. I had a wonderful dad, but he died. I don't know what's worse. My mom is great, though."

They perused the photographs a while longer, Carmen talking about happy times with her grandmother. "This was a trip to the zoo, obviously, with the elephants and all. This one was taken at the lake, while fishing with Grandpa. That was the biggest fish I ever caught. He said he called the fish to come just for me." She laughed. "He was funny." Carmen recalled that after her grandfather's comment, she beckoned the ducks to come to her. But she kept her powers a secret, as her mother had told her to.

She felt much better after cuddling beside him. He let her talk and never made her feel silly for her emotions.

"I have to let the dog out, but I can come back, if you want," Peter said.

"No, it's okay. I feel ready to sleep now."

"Okay. Good night, then." He kissed her. "Call me if you change your mind."

Carmen made sure that she had locked all the windows and doors, again, and proceeded to bed. She was surprised that she wasn't afraid to be alone in her house anymore. She knew she could handle anyone that trespassed, and she would gladly handle them her way.

At work the next day, Carmen kept to herself. She wasn't in the mood to socialize. She did her job, not putting too much of herself into it, and she didn't go out of her way to help anyone.

Why bother? she thought. *I'm fed up with being judge and jury. I don't even put a dent into the injustice that goes on everywhere. And who's looking out for me? Nobody! I am annoyed with it all. Everyone, just leave me alone and do whatever you want.*

She picked up a takeout dinner after her shift and went straight home to eat it by the TV. She looked for a show to cheer her up, but nothing worked, and the commercials promising results that by no means occurred just added to the misery.

The news caught her attention when the anchor mentioned that the police had found the owner of the green minivan. Just as Carmen had intended, the driver slammed into a light post. The police found a sweater belonging to one of the children and hairs from another in the back of the van and were searching for its owner, whose name and address they had. *Good. Bastard*, Carmen thought, still not feeling any better.

She turned off the TV and went out for a walk. She stopped to pet one of the neighbour's cats when he rubbed up against her leg and purred. She scratched him behind his ears, and her disposition softened a little. It was a beautiful night; the air was so fresh. She took a deep breath, closing her eyes to feel it. The cat sauntered off to find someone else's leg to nestle up to.

The young man next door avoided her. *Strange*, she

realized. He always came over to talk to her. He took off with a bunch of other men, laughing and pushing each other. How different people were when they were in groups.

Carmen got halfway around the block when she noticed a mother bird feeding her baby on someone's lawn. The baby bird squawked for food, and the mother did what her instinct told her to do to keep the species going, attending to the annoying little demands and caring for the baby, even sacrificing herself for it.

Carmen walked on and saw an old couple. The man, so frail himself, was helping his tiny wife down the steps of the bakery. The little woman smiled at Carmen. "He's still my knight in shining armour," she boasted.

Carmen softened. She could have kicked herself for her behaviour today. She knew there were still a lot of good people in the world, and they needed her. They hadn't all let her down.

"I'm sorry," she said to herself.

"What's that, dear?" the elderly gentleman asked.

"Thank you," she answered, and then she blessed them both with relief from their aches and pains.

She headed home and arrived just in time to answer the phone. It was Peter.

"I didn't see you at all today," Carmen said. "Didn't you work?"

"I did, but the MRI machine was acting funny today," Peter replied. "That kept me busy and in one area all day. The department had to reschedule a bunch of appointments, but we did get it working right again. I missed seeing you today."

"I think it was better that you didn't see me." Carmen snickered.

"What? Why would you say that?"

"Because I was in a bad mood."

"As a result of the break-in the other day?" Peter guessed.

"Primarily, yes," Carmen answered, somewhat embarrassed about the truth.

"I'm sorry. I was under the impression that you felt better by the time I left your place last night," Peter said sadly.

"I did, but then this morning, it hit me again."

"Are you feeling better now?"

"Yes. It took a walk around the block to bring me back to my senses."

"Good," he said. "I have to go now. My mom left a message for me to call her."

"Wow, you called me before your mother?"

"Yes, but don't let that go to your head. And don't tell her!" Peter hung up.

Carmen smiled peacefully and prepared herself for bed.

Peter called his mother as she had asked him to. He was tired, so he tried to keep it short, but that was difficult with mothers sometimes.

"I haven't heard from you for a while," Rachel Anderson said. "So I decided that I would call, but then you weren't home. What is keeping you so busy? A girl, I hope," she jested with a little glimmer of sincerity.

"Actually, Mom, there is a girl. A woman, I mean. I've known her for a while, but we've just recently started dating. I might have mentioned her before. Carmen? She's an RN at work."

"I remember. You have talked about her for years. I told you long ago to ask her out. But instead, you got hooked up with that grocery store clerk, and then the one from the cable company, and then—"

"Yes, Mom, I get the idea," Peter interrupted. "I know I've had too many relationships that didn't pan out. But, it's hard to ask out an RN. I mean, she's an RN. They usually date the doctors."

"You are a smart, handsome, wonderful man. Just like your father. You are a great catch for any woman, even a registered nurse. Now, tell me more about her."

"I'm really tired. Can we finish this another time?"

"What, you just throw out the bait and then reel it back in?"

"Yup, just like fly fishing." Peter laughed.

"Oh, now I'm a fish?" Rachel grumbled.

"No, Mom. Of course not. I'm just tired. The MRI machine was—"

"If you have time to talk about MRI machines, I would much rather hear about this woman. Have you taken her out? Where? When did you start seeing her?"

"I asked her out last week. We went to the record store, then to dinner the next night."

"Where did you take her for dinner?"

"Don't worry, Mom. It wasn't fast food. I took her to Bella Italia."

"Oh, wonderful! That place is so quaint, and by the way, I didn't think you would take her for fast food. I know you have class because I raised you well. So, do you like her?"

"Yes. I wouldn't take her out if I didn't like her," Peter answered.

"Don't get snippy. I mean do you *really* like her?" Rachel persisted.

"I'm sorry, Mom. I'm tired. I didn't mean to sound snippy. Yes, I really like her."

"It's okay, sweetie. You go to bed. I'll do the same and dream of my future grandchildren." She chuckled as she blew Peter a kiss through the phone.

Peter loved his mom. She was great. He could not wait to tell her more about Carmen. He was sure she would like her. Why wouldn't she? Carmen was incredible. Too bad Peter's dad wasn't still alive to meet her too.

3

The next day, Carmen and Peter went for a drive to enjoy the countryside in the sunshine.

They drove along the river and stopped at a breathtaking waterfall, Tiffany Falls, set back in the forest. *What a perfect place for a romantic kiss*, Carmen thought. *I've been here before, but I've never been kissed here before.* She laughed inside at the little verse. She and Peter talked and laughed. They walked the path that twisted between the boulders. Moss grew on the damp rocks near the falls, and the mist sparkled in their hair.

Peter had brought his dog on their excursion. Shelley was a little Sheltie, full of life and curiosity. She chased a squirrel through the forest but came back immediately when Peter called her. Carmen liked her, and she liked Carmen too. When they first met this morning, Shelley had licked Carmen's hand and wagged her tail frantically.

Animals, including the squirrels, birds and chipmunks around her house, sensed something different about

Carmen, and she felt like they accepted her. She wished that people were so easy to get along with.

Shelley didn't seem the least bit jealous of Carmen. She ran around their legs, looking up at them periodically as they walked along.

They stood on a small bridge watching the falls. "My mom is great," Peter said, when Carmen asked. "She's retired but was a biochemist for her entire career. She is very smart and wise. She has always supported me. She started an education fund for me when I was small, and all I ever wanted to be was an engineer. I was always building things and taking things apart to see how they worked. I took the VCR apart when I was a kid. She was really mad at first, but she was impressed when I put it back together and played a movie on it. She pushed me to the right career. I worked for a water filtration company for a while, but then I heard about an opening at the hospital, and here I am."

"You are lucky to have had so much support," Carmen said. "Tell me about your dad."

"Dad was just as awesome as Mom, and they were so much in love. They played and teased each other and worked together. He was a pharmacist and owned the pharmacy beside the Chinese market. He died several years ago of cancer. Mom was broken-hearted, but I tried to support her despite my own sadness. My uncle Joe, Dad's brother, has been a blessing to us. I'd like you to meet my mother, if it isn't too soon."

"I'd like that."

"Good. Well, that's enough about me. What about you?" Peter asked.

"I told you a bit about my parents. They weren't role models like yours were. I have a younger sister, Jill, who is married with children. I went to university right out of high school and got my nursing license. I moved out as soon as I got a job. I worked first for a family doctor, but he moved to the States. I didn't want to go with him, so he gave me a reference, and I applied at the hospital."

"Did you always want to be a nurse?"

"As long as I can remember."

"Why? Although I can picture you as a little girl taking care of your dolls."

Carmen had chosen nursing because it allowed her to use her powers, but she quickly thought of her other reasons. "I always wanted to help people." It sounded so cliché, but she wasn't ready to tell Peter of her powers. She had lost boyfriends before when she told them.

The trail took them full circle back to the car. Shelley got in obediently, and like any dog, she stuck her head out the window, sniffing the breeze as they drove.

A car sped past them going much too fast. "Gee, what a nut," Peter said. "He's just asking for an accident. He may not care about his own life, but he sure could hurt someone else."

Carmen agreed and tried to think of a way to slow the idiot down. A flat tire might make him crash, and she didn't want that, but running out of gas would slow him right down. She concentrated on her plan. Further along the road, they came upon the stalled car, its driver irate. Retribution achieved.

Peter seemed quite satisfied. "Well," he said. "That's what I call just deserts."

He just might become my partner in crime. Should I tell him that I caused that? He might suggest ideas. This could be fun.

As they continued their travels, Carmen watched the landscape blur by, lost in memories of her troubled childhood. Her powers had created much conflict within her. She could hear her classmates' taunts almost as vividly as she had when she was just a girl.

"Carmen, A plus. As usual, good job."

"As usual, good job," Robbie parroted in a nasal voice.

"Teacher's pet," the girl behind her said.

"Smarty pants," another child added.

"What did you do, Carmen? Why is Robbie's nose bleeding? Weird stuff always happens when you're around."

Carmen snapped back to the present. *I am not going to tell him anything!*

Peter and Carmen finished their adventure with a cup of tea at Carmen's house. Meanwhile, Shelley explored every room. She stopped at the back door and barked. When Carmen let her out, the young man next door asked if she had gotten a dog.

"No she isn't mine, Allan. She's Peter's dog. Allan, this is Peter Anderson, my coworker and friend. Peter, this is Allan Roberts, my neighbour."

"Oh. Hi," Allan said quickly, and he turned to go back inside.

"He seemed nervous, don't you think?" Peter said.

"He's been like that a couple of days now," Carmen observed.

"So am I only your coworker and friend?" he interrogated.

"I don't know. What do you think that you are?" She leaned against the railing of her deck.

"I'd like to think that I might be your boyfriend by now." Peter looked up and put an ear to his shoulder coyly.

Carmen laughed. "Okay, you can be my boyfriend."

Shelley, as if she understood, bounced joyously at their feet. They went back inside.

"Hey, Shelley," Carmen said, "how would you like to spend the night? And your daddy can stay, too, so you won't be scared."

"Oh, so she'll sleep in your bed and I'll sleep on the floor. Or will it be the other way around?"

"You know, I have a feeling both of you will be in my bed tonight." Carmen laughed.

She had the next day to herself since Peter was booked to work. It was good that she wasn't, because she figured she would be in la-la land and smirking all day.

Their lovemaking had been magical. Carmen had only dreamed that it could be like that. He was warm and gentle, slow and giving. Peter looked incredible, felt incredible, and smelled incredible. He just *was* incredible. He said and did all the right things.

The dog had been silly at first but then was lulled to sleep by the gentle rocking of the bed.

In the morning, Carmen made breakfast while Peter showered. He came downstairs sexier than ever in his jeans, black shirt, and bare feet. Oh, how she loved a guy in jeans and bare feet. He ran his hands through his wet curly hair and over the one-day's worth of stubble on his face.

He put one arm around her waist and the other around her shoulder, pulled her close, and kissed her fervently. His mouth slid to her neck, and she felt tingles throughout her body.

"Don't start what you can't finish," she stated.

He agreed, ran both his hands through his hair, and sighed heavily. "Last night was so amazing."

She nodded, smiled, and placed his breakfast in front of him. "Absolutely."

After breakfast, Peter kissed her goodbye at the door. "I could get used to this."

"I could too," Carmen responded.

"Be a good girl," he said to Shelley. "Stay." She whimpered. "It's okay. You'll stay with Carmen today."

After he left, Carmen took Shelley for a walk, as she had promised she would, and they headed in the opposite direction from the hospital, toward the busier part of town.

Carmen she saw a woman hail a taxi, but then a man ran over and opened the door on the other side of the car. "Oh no, you don't." Carmen flung her arm, sending a vibration through space toward the man, sending his hat flying off his head and down the road. He ran after it, allowing the woman to get into the cab that she had hailed.

Shelley looked up at Carmen and barked. Did she

know? She could probably feel the force that Carmen had used. "It's okay, Shelley. I won't hurt you."

They continued toward the flower shop, passing two children fighting over a red lollipop. The bigger child pulled it away from the smaller one. Carmen interceded, and an invisible force caused the child to lose her grip on the lollipop, leaving it in the hand of the smaller child. The bigger child looked behind her, of course seeing no one there. The mother looked perplexed. Carmen, thinking that the mother should have intervened herself, caused the woman's coffee to splash her shirt. "That oughta teach you."

In the tiny flower shop, Carmen and Shelley enjoyed the fragrances. "Which ones should we get, Shelley?" The little canine stuck her nose into a bunch of purple violets. "Oh, yes. Good choice, Shelley!"

Carmen turned to the owner. "We'll take those, Anne." They conversed for a short time, and then Carmen and Shelley were on their way.

"Wanna go to the pet shop, pretty girl? I bet we can find you a nice biscuit."

Shelley wagged her tail and pulled on her leash toward the store next to the flower shop. They went inside, wafted by various natural smells. The dog stuck her nose in the air and sniffed, pulling Carmen toward the bunnies in the display pen. "Do you like bunnies, puppy? They are cute, aren't they? But you are more fun."

Carmen found some treats and a rubber ball and proceeded to the front counter. The girl there was too busy texting to care for her customers. Carmen interrupted her with an ahem, but the girl continued to type. When she looked up, Carmen manipulated the cell phone's battery to drain completely, leaving the girl with nothing to do but her job. Cause and effect.

Shelley barked.

They continued on, Shelley right at Carmen's side. "You're a good girl, aren't you? You don't pull at all. Peter sure trained you well. I really like your daddy, Shelley. I hope you don't mind sharing him, because I'd really like to be a part of your lives."

The pet looked up at her, wagged her tail and offered a double bark.

"I'll take that as a yes." Carmen rubbing the pup on the head. "Let's get a drink. I'm thirsty. There's a café up here that has a little doggy dish too."

A little further up the street, they reached a quaint teashop with bistro tables on the sidewalk, wisteria along the back of the patio and strings of lights coiled around the old-fashioned street lamps. Sure enough, the doggy dish was full of water for the patrons' furry friends. Shelley lapped up her fill, and Carmen ordered an iced tea. It came in a tall, frosty glass with a lemon slice wedged on the rim and a plastic straw with a blue swirl.

"This quenches my thirst," Carmen mentioned to the pooch. "We'll sit for a few minutes and then head back to my house." The dog crawled under the table to lie in the shade and rested her head on Carmen's feet. "I approve of you too, little one." How happy she felt.

Her cell phone rang. It was Peter on his coffee break. "How are my two lovely girls doing?"

"We are having a grand time together," Carmen replied. "Just stopped at the Teetotalers' Tea Shop for an iced tea. Anything you want while we're out?"

"Well, let's see … I'd like a beautiful woman with a great body, luxurious dark hair, full lips and sexy legs. Do you think Shelley can drag her home for me?"

"I doubt it. I'm holding her leash pretty tightly, so she'd never be able to get away to find a woman like that." She laughed.

"Ha, ha. You know I meant you!" He snorted.

Was this guy for real? Carmen pinched herself to make sure she wasn't dreaming.

"I have to get back to work. Get home safely, okay?" he said.

On the way home, on the opposite side of the street, Carmen noticed the little pharmacy beside the Chinese market. She tried to remember if she had ever been in there and met Peter's father. She usually used the pharmacy near the hospital. *Gee, maybe I could have met Peter sooner if I had gone to this pharmacy. Oh well, what can you do?*

They did get home safely. Shelley ate her biscuit while Carmen made dinner. She put a whole chicken garnished and flavoured with fresh rosemary from her garden into the oven. Shelley had played in the backyard and come back to smell the rosemary when Carmen snipped it off the plant. She gave out a cute little sneeze as if she had inhaled the savoury herb too briskly. Carmen laughed.

She also oven roasted some potatoes with paprika, garlic and olive oil. Fresh beans were rinsed and placed in the steamer, which was to be turned on a little later.

Peter came home to an aromatic house. He came to her, grasped her by the waist and said, "Not only did Shelley bring home that beautiful woman with a great body, luxurious dark hair, full lips and sexy legs that I asked for, but she brought home a chef. It smells great in here."

"Thanks, how was work?"

"The usual." He reached into his pocket. "I imagined you might like this." He gave her a little paper bag.

Carmen accepted it, smiling. "For me? What a nice surprise." She opened it, looked at Peter and reached inside the bag. She pulled out a fine metal bookmark etched with the words, "God bless nurses, for they have love to share, compassion to care and kindness to spare."

"This is beautiful. Thank you, Peter." She stretched up to kiss him.

"There's one more thing in there." He indicated the bag.

"Oh." She turned it over and a fridge magnet tumbled out. She managed to catch it before it fell to the floor. Inscribed on it was the message, "I am a superhero cleverly disguised as a nurse." Carmen laughed. *If you only knew.*

"It isn't much, but I saw them in the gift shop at the hospital and thought they were appropriate for you."

Carmen looked at him. *Does he know? Have I slipped?* "Oh, because I'm a nurse." She turned on the stove to steam the vegetables.

"Of course. What else? Silly."

Geez, stop being so jumpy. "Dinner is ready," Carmen said as she put the magnet on the fridge.

"Great. The smell made me hungry." Peter reached for the dinner plates. Shelley followed him. "What are you going to eat, Shelley? I guess I should buy a bag of your food to keep here, if that's okay with Carmen."

"Sure. Bring your stuff, too. Toothbrush, whatever. I don't mind." Carmen imagined them living in the same house. Whose would it be? It would be best to buy a new one together, a fresh start. A house in the country with chickens, rabbits, a goat, another dog for Shelley, cats. Carmen drifted off to fantasyland while she reached for the roasted potatoes and burned her hand on the side of the oven.

"Ouch!" she blurted out in pain. She put the casserole dish down on the trivet and clenched the burn. She turned on the cold water tap and immersed her hand in the stream.

"Are you all right?" Peter asked. "What happened?"

Carmen had already willed the burn to heal and then drained the sink. "Nothing, I'm fine."

"But you hurt yourself. Was it a burn? Let me see," Peter insisted.

Carmen turned toward the table in frustration. "I'm fine."

"Then why did you have it in cold water? Gee, Carmen, just because you're the nurse it doesn't mean that *you* don't need to be cared for occasionally." He grabbed her hands and turned them over and back again. "There's nothing there."

"I told you."

"Then why the ouch and the cold water?"

"Peter, please. I'm fine. Let's eat." *Man, he doesn't give up easily, does he?*

Peter still looked peeved.

The subject was dropped for the rest of the evening, but Peter's suspicion had worried Carmen. He had not just accepted that there was no injury to her hand. If she didn't tell him about her secret, he might find out for himself. In the meantime, she would have to be more careful.

After dinner, Peter went home and made up a bag of things to leave at Carmen's house. He put in an extra toothbrush from the dentist and a new deodorant. He then looked at pajamas and decided not to bother. He grinned. He didn't have an extra comb, but he could get one.

He fed the cat. "You probably like the peace and quiet, don't you, Oscar?" Then he grabbed a zippered plastic bag of Shelley's food and returned to Carmen's.

Carmen and Peter rose in the morning to the whimpering of a dog with a full bladder. "Okay, Shelley, let's go," Peter said.

"Can I take her? Will you go with me, Shelley?"

Shelley ran downstairs, and Carmen staggered out of the bedroom and down after her. She let the dog out. It was a beautiful fresh morning with a slight breeze. The birds were singing their hearts out. Shelley ran around looking for a spot that she liked, but with so many new smells, she took a little longer than usual.

"Come on, Shelley," Carmen called when Shelley had finished. The dog came in and ran ahead of her. Carmen shut the door and then returned upstairs.

"Would you like me to hang back so you can get ready without me in your way?" Peter asked. "I can lock up after you leave."

"Sure. I should give you my spare key then." She got the key for him, and he accepted it. *That is a step forward,* she thought.

The hospital could be a very hectic place. It was full of nurses, visitors, doctors, physiotherapists, dieticians, housekeepers, kitchen staff, pharmacy techs, and on and on. The nurses' station was especially crowded, and staff bumped into each other as they attended to ringing phones, computers and charts. The nurses were always kept busy by patients requesting things, family asking questions, doctors wanting information, and piles of charting. Carmen loved every minute of it.

She loved the fast pace with constant stimulation and not a moment for boredom. The interaction with people was her favourite part of her job. She loved cheering her patients up, sometimes with something as simple as a heated blanket. If she could not answer a question, she would find the answer. Her coworkers—well, most of them—respected her, and she was worthy of their respect. She was hard-working, honest, ethical, caring, accommodating and patient.

Carmen watched Lisa Kerrigan, another nurse, do

her job. She loved Lisa's manner with her patients, even though she hadn't had it easy lately since she had found out her boyfriend was cheating on her. No amount of reassurance, such as, "Well, at least you found out before you were married to him," could ease her pain. Carmen wished she could meet the cheating jerk just long enough to curse him with something like baldness or impotence. Harsh, maybe, but watching Lisa suffer made her irate. In addition, well, tit for tat.

Lisa was a cute, blonde, twenty-four-year-old, less experienced nurse whom Carmen had taken under her wing. She had been Lisa's preceptor when Lisa had still been in training, and she had recommended that the manager hire her.

Carmen fabricated a pretty white rosebud and left it on Lisa's medication cart in the hallway. Then she went in the patient's room to see if Lisa needed any help since Carmen's own patients were all having an after-lunch nap. Lisa accepted the help, and they conversed while they cared for the unresponsive patient.

"Rumour has it that you and Peter Anderson are dating," Lisa said.

"Gossip rushes through here like wildfire," Carmen responded.

"So it's true?" Lisa asked.

"Yes, it is true, and it isn't some sordid affair. I believe we have a future together."

"Well, I think it is great," Lisa admitted. "I think Peter is a decent guy."

"I'm crazy about him," Carmen divulged.

Just as Carmen and Lisa were finishing with the patient, Betty barged in to tell Carmen that her patient at the other end of the hall wanted more pain medication.

"Certainly. I'll get him something," Carmen responded.

"Now, why couldn't she have just given him something herself instead of taking the time to search for you?" Lisa asked when Betty had left.

"Because that's just the way she is. I think it makes her feel like she's showing me that I'm not taking good care of my patients. I can handle her. She's just like my mother."

Lisa looked astonished. "Poor you. Do you think she overheard us talking about you and Peter?"

"I don't know, but if she did, the news will travel even faster than wildfire now, and it'll be completely altered."

By the end of the shift, Carmen's feet burned and her legs throbbed. She had confessed to Lisa that the rosebud was from her. She surely didn't want Lisa to think that she had a guy to wonder about. "I just wanted you to know what a great nurse you've become," she admitted.

Lisa's eyes welled up. "Thanks, Carmen. That means a lot to me."

"You deserve it. Lord knows, we're always told what we're doing wrong, so we should pat each other on the back for what we're doing right."

They walked out of the building together but then parted when they reached the street.

Peter pulled up in his car and offered Carmen a ride home, and she accepted, telling him how much her feet hurt.

When they reached her house, she invited him inside. He looked like he wanted to ask her something.

"What is it?" she asked.

"What?" he replied stupidly.

"You look like you want to spill the beans, so spill them."

"I want to ask you something," he said seriously.

They had put away their coats, so she directed him to the couch. "It sounds serious," Carmen said softly.

"I'd like you to meet my mother. She asked me to come to dinner Saturday night and said she'd like you to come." He sounded relieved when he finished.

"You've mentioned me to your mother?" Carmen asked hopefully.

"Well, kind of. My mother has a way of pulling information right out of me." Peter laughed.

"Don't they all?" Carmen nudged him with her shoulder and laughed with him. "I already told you that I would meet her. And don't worry; I'll be on my best behaviour." She laughed again.

They sat down for leftover chicken.

"Oh, and how about tomorrow you come to my place so I can cook dinner for you?" Peter suggested. "You'll see that I'm not useless in the kitchen."

"Well, if you're half as good in the kitchen as you are in the bedroom, I'd love to come over."

They slept in their own beds that night.

Peter had spent the day cleaning his house and

shopping for the ingredients for his favourite dish, chicken-and-biscuit pie. It was his mom's recipe, handed down from her mother. It always reminded him of home.

Shelley had enjoyed having him at home and charmed him with her big brown eyes into taking her in the car to the grocery store. He had made the dough for the green onion biscuits first and then boiled the chicken. Shelley was going crazy by then. He gave her a piece of chicken and then continued his culinary adventure by making the sauce. He now had the casserole ready for the oven but wouldn't put it in until Carmen arrived. He had made a garden salad, a pickle tray and rice pudding, but he had already selected a red wine.

He went upstairs to clean himself up so he looked his best for her. He brushed his teeth, used mouthwash, shaved for the second time today, and headed back downstairs after donning a blue-and-grey plaid shirt. He left two buttons undone. He coordinated the golf shirt with black chinos and a black belt. Shelley had followed him upstairs, so he gave her a light brushing as well.

"Do we look presentable, girl?" he asked his faithful friend with a pat on her head. She licked his hand. "I think so too."

Peter's cat woke with the intrusion and stretched before jumping off the bed to rub up against his leg. "I bet you smell the chicken too, don't you, goofy?" The cat meowed and then swatted at Shelley when she came too close. "Gee, Oscar, what are we going to do with all these girls in our life?"

The doorbell rang. Peter was relieved that his

directions had been accurate. He ran downstairs, followed by his two furry friends. When he opened the door, the cat shot outside.

It surprised Carmen.

"That's Oscar. The more the merrier!" Peter said. "I'm a sucker for wet noses. Come on in and join the zoo." He stepped back to allow her to come in.

"It smells good in here! What a nice place you have," Carmen added, looking around.

Peter's house was masculine but not a man cave. Like Carmen, he had leather furniture, but it was beige, and a sectional. He had placed a large wooden cocktail table in front of the couch and heavy glass end tables on one end of the sectional and beside one chair.

The dining room had been decorated with parson's chairs in black leather and a dining table in the same wood as the cocktail table. He had chosen California shutters for the windows and had placed simple but heavy accents on the mantle and tables. There were two plants by the sliding glass doors that lead to the patio.

The kitchen had black cupboards, stainless-steel appliances and a cork floor.

"Your place is very classy," Carmen said. "We have the same taste, don't we?"

"That's what I was thinking when I first saw your place," Peter professed.

Shelley, wanting to be noticed, barked at Carmen and then sat and waited for her acknowledgement.

Carmen knelt and patted the dog's head, asking if she remembered her.

"How could she forget you after the outing you had the other day?" Peter said. *I couldn't forget you either*, he thought. *You are all I think about.* He kissed her quickly, grabbed her hand and added, "Come into the kitchen. I have to put dinner in the oven."

"Can I help you with anything?" Carmen offered.

"No, thanks. It's all ready to go. I've been slaving over a hot stove all day." He dramatically wiped his brow with the back of his hand. "You look very nice, by the way. Did you change at the hospital or work in that all day?" He laughed at himself.

"Oh, yeah, sure, I worked all day in this outfit and it still looks and smells fresh," she mocked.

"You smell good to me." Peter nuzzled his nose into her neck. The dog tilted her head at them.

"Stop that," Carmen said, putting her hands in front of her hips. "Not in front of the children."

They both laughed. "Don't teach the birds and the bees to the dogs and the cats," Peter said as he led her to the patio. They sat outside watching the birds tease the dog. Peter took the cellophane off the platter of devilled eggs he had set out and offered them to her.

"Gee, I haven't had devilled eggs for ages. I love them." Carmen accepted one of the slippery eggs and attempted to bite it in half rather than shove the whole thing in her mouth. She managed to balance the rest on her fingertips. "Hey, these are especially good. Do you have a secret ingredient?"

"It's so secret that I have it locked away." He imitated pulling a zipper across his lips and turning a key.

"Oh, my goodness. Do you have secrets already?" Carmen laughed, but then she remembered her own.

Shelley brought her ball to Peter, wiggling in anticipation. He threw it, and she ran after it as fast as she could. She caught it before it hit the ground and brought it right back to Peter to begin all over again. They did this a few times, and then Carmen threw it too. Shelley panted heavily, and Peter told her that was enough. "I'm trying to visit with Carmen, and you just keep interrupting."

After some socializing, the timer for the oven went off. "Dinner is ready," Peter chimed. "I hope you like it. It's my favourite. My mom used to make it."

"I hope I like it too," Carmen jested. "I'm hungry and wouldn't want to have to wait for takeout."

Peter made a raspberry at her with his tongue.

"Don't worry. I'll eat it even if I don't like it. My mom raised me that way. I couldn't leave the table if I didn't eat what she made."

"You've been vague about your mother. How is your relationship with her?"

"We never really saw eye to eye."

"What do you mean?"

"She tried to control me and restrain me, and I think that was because she was ashamed of me." Carmen's eyes moistened.

"What? How can a mother be ashamed of her child?" Peter asked.

"Because, I'm different." A tear ran down Carmen's cheek.

"Bullshit! You are exceptional!" Peter said angrily.

"I don't want to talk about this." She choked on her words.

"Okay, this is too upsetting for you." He stepped toward her, lifted her face with one finger, and kissed her on her nose.

"Was this your favourite dish when you were little?" Carmen asked.

Peter scooped some onto her plate. "I can remember liking this when I was small."

Carmen let the casserole cool and then took a bite. "It's good."

Peter nodded. "Mom taught me how to make it when I was a teen. When Dad died we worked together in the kitchen."

Supper was a big success, and Peter's cooking impressed Carmen. The rest of the evening was pleasant and relaxing.

She had to work the next day, so she didn't stay too late. As she left, the cat returned.

As Carmen stepped around the hedge, she decided she would get home faster over the rooftops, and she would be hidden in the darkness, so she floated up onto the neighbour's roof and leapt onto the next toward home. At one house, she had to duck behind the shed to avoid being noticed by the stargazers in the yard, but she got home without making the morning news.

4

The thief headed to the other end of town with his bounty. He had stashed the small things in a backpack and boarded the downtown bus. He fit in just fine with the riff-raff of that neighbourhood. His mother had raised him in a decent part of town, but since his dad walked out, he had become involved with reprobates.

He fooled the adults most of the time, coming across as a decent kid. They even felt sorry for him because his father had left. Little did they know he took things right from under their noses. He had his mother fooled too. She was under the impression that he was a normal kid who argued with his mother. But she had no idea what he was capable of. She didn't catch that money went missing from her wallet; he took just enough that she wouldn't notice. She would have been broken-hearted if she knew.

He reached the pawnshop and dumped the contents of his bag onto the counter. "I have some stuff I want to sell."

"Where did you get these things?" asked the storeowner.

"My grandmother died, and me and my mom don't want none of it."

"I'll need to look these things over. They're old." He could see some of them were valuable, and something rang familiar to him. "I can give you a hundred bucks for the lot." He picked up his notebook and went to the till. The phone rang. "Hang on."

He answered the phone. "I don't have any right now, but they come in a lot. Nevertheless, they go almost as fast. No … well, they range in price depending …"

The shop owner kept an eye on the young man while he spoke and noticed him drumming his fingers on the counter and sweating. He assumed that the man just wanted to get rid of the stuff and get out of there.

The store owner hung up and came back to the items on the counter. Then it hit him: he'd seen these items in the pictures of vintage jewellery that the young woman who'd been robbed had brought in. "Hey, man, I want to give you a fair price, and I think this stuff might be worth something. Can you leave it with me so I can have a friend of mine look it over?"

"I don't want to come back," the young man said. "Give me two hundred and I'll call it fair."

"Oh, I don't know." He had to stall, and a name, address and phone number would be great for the police. How could he call them and keep the man here? *I know.* "Let me see if my buddy can come over now." He hurried to the back and called 9-1-1 from his cell phone.

The young man's greed did him in. He waited until not the appraiser but the police came, and he was arrested.

Carmen was still at work when the police called her to say that they had found her grandmother's jewellery. She was elated. "What luck! I never thought I would see those things again. Where did you find them?" she inquired.

"At the King Street Pawn Shop," the Desk Sergeant answered. "The owner called it in today while the guy was still in the store. He remembered you and recognized the jewellery in the pictures. What an idiot the guy was to try to pawn these things off."

"I'm lucky that he's an idiot," Carmen replied. "Can I come in after I finish work?"

They made the arrangements for her to at least identify the pieces, and Carmen went back to work in a very good mood. She had a skip in her step as she checked on her patients.

On her break, she called Peter to tell him the good news. He was happy for her.

"Do you want me to go with you tonight?" he suggested.

She accepted his offer and checked the clock to see how much longer it was until they would go. *Just a couple of hours,* she realized.

When Carmen and Peter had finished work, they met in the parking garage as arranged. Peter drove. They had to deal with some traffic on the way to the police station at the other end of town, but they still got there in decent time. Carmen was anxious to get her things back, although she knew that the police had to process the evidence.

At the station, they asked for Sergeant Campbell. When he came to the desk, he greeted Carmen and Peter with a friendly smile with crooked teeth. He was a stout man with a full head of white hair and thick, curly eyebrows. Then came the grand Scottish accent, thick as all get-out, as the Scottish people say. "What kinna do fer ya?"

"I am Carmen Hamilton. You called me about the jewellery you confiscated at the King Street Pawnshop." She shook his outstretched hand.

"Ah yes, come with me," the Sergeant said as he opened the gate to the area behind the desk. I'd like you to see if you can identify the man who stole your things." He led them to the small office and pulled out a file. "It was a great idea to bring in the pictures of your jewellery to the pawn shop. The owner of the store recognized your items. Otherwise, he might have just bought them, sold them, and you'd never see them again.

"We have the young man in custody, and it would be safer for you to see him through the one-way glass. We have the jewellery for you to identify as well."

Peter went with Carmen to the one-way glass. He touched her arm reassuringly as she looked at the man sitting in the interrogation room. Carmen gasped, looked closer, squeezed her eyes shut and then looked at the man again. "That's Allan Roberts!"

"Aye," the Sergeant said.

"Who's Allan Roberts?" Peter asked.

"My neighbour," Carmen said.

"The one you introduced me to the other day?" Peter asked.

"Yes. No wonder he's been acting strangely lately. But why would he steal from me? I've always been nice to him. I thought we got along okay …" She trailed off sadly.

"We are charging him with theft," the Sergeant said. "We will need your jewellery as evidence, but you will eventually get it back."

"What about all her other things?" Peter inquired.

"We've already applied for a warrant to search his house for the other things that were missing from Carmen's home."

"So he's the one who climbed through my window," Carmen said. "He would have seen that it was open and that I wasn't home. Maybe he even watched me leave." She became angrier with every word she spoke. "I was irate that I had been robbed, but now I am livid that I was robbed by someone I know. Neighbours are supposed to look out for each other, not rob each other!"

She identified the jewellery as hers and said that she thought all the pieces were there. She was too angry to notice the extra necklace in the batch.

Peter helped her get up. "Come on. Let's get you home." He turned to the Sergeant. "Is that all you need from us now?"

"Aye. I'm sorry, Miss Hamilton, but this will all work out. You were very lucky to have found your jewellery," Sergeant Campbell said, rolling his *r*'s. "Usually, people who have been robbed never see their things again. Roberts was just a stupid criminal."

Carmen barely heard him; she was already thinking

of the punishment she wanted to inflict on Allan Roberts. *Live by the sword, die by the sword.*

As Peter drove Carmen home, he asked if she was all right.

"I'm hurt," she said.

"I can understand that completely." He rubbed her arm and gave her a half-hearted smile. "I wouldn't expect anything else." .

She fell silent again. Just like when she first saw her house had been ransacked, she wanted to withdraw again. She apologized to Peter. He was so supportive and agreeable.

At home, Peter poured Carmen a glass of wine and tucked her under a blanket on the couch. "Do you want me to stay or go?"

"I want you to stay. Make me feel better. Help me understand."

"I'll try." He sat beside her and suggested that the TV might help them escape for a while. They found an uplifting program that helped to restore her hope in humanity. Peter helped, too. She even laughed a little.

"I need to forgive him. We all do things wrong sometimes. I know I do, too," Carmen confessed. She took the last sip from her glass and rested it on the table.

"That is a great attitude, Carmen."

She felt much calmer now. She yawned, and Peter said that he should go. "Will you be all right? Do you need anything?" He tucked the blanket around her again.

"I'm fine," she said and walked him to the door. They noticed the police were at the Roberts' house. "His poor mother."

Peter kissed her warmly and reminded her to lock the door. She watched the police for a minute more and then heated some soup before heading to bed. By then, the police had left.

Carmen lay awake for a while until the stillness and darkness lulled her to sleep.

I need a vacation, she thought the next morning. *I'm going to try to get some time off work. A change of scenery would be just the trick. It would be nice to bring Peter, but I don't know if he can get time off too. I could get a doctor's note, but he couldn't.*

Maybe a visit to Jill's place would be a good idea. I haven't seen her for a long time, and sisters shouldn't be apart that long.

Although Jill was Carmen's younger sister, she was already married to Gary Patterson, and they had two children. They lived only a couple hours away. Jill knew Carmen better than anyone did and loved her unconditionally, just as Carmen loved her. They didn't talk enough. Carmen didn't want to intrude on her busy life. *But if I go there, I can help her out a bit. Yes! That is exactly what I'll do.*

Carmen planned to arrange for a week off, beginning on Saturday. There were some part-timers crying for more hours, so it wouldn't be a problem. She would meet Peter's mother on Saturday evening and then go to Jill's on Sunday morning. Should she call Jill or surprise her? *I know: I'll arrange it with Gary but then surprise Jill.*

If Jill answered the phone, Carmen would tell her that she called just to chat, but if Gary answered, she would ask about a visit. Luckily, Gary answered the phone. Jill was picking up their daughter, Jessica, from a play date.

Their son, Bradley, was home with Gary, so Gary went to the other room to talk. Bradley was only five and would surely spill the beans to his mother if he overheard.

Gary thought the visit was a great idea. He told Carmen that just the other day, Jill had been saying that they needed to catch up. He loved the idea of a surprise. "Of course, she'll probably freak that she didn't clean up before you came, but she'll love the visit."

Carmen told Gary that she had been robbed and that she needed a change of scenery to destress.

He was surprised and told her he was sorry. He couldn't believe it when she told him who the thief was. "Rotten jack-ass," he said supportively. "Some people just have the audacity, don't they? Well, you come on over and find some peace here."

So, she arranged to go on Sunday morning, and Gary said he would make sure that Jill didn't go anywhere.

Carmen felt excited and already felt some of the stress fall off her shoulders.

She remembered how Jill had been there for her. As the younger child, she thought Carmen's gift was cool. She looked up to Carmen and even tried to get her to fight some battles for her. Of course, as a big sister, Carmen did.

There had been a time in middle school when a girl in Jill's class tripped Jill and made her fall in the mud in front of the boys. The bully had tormented her, so Carmen went with Jill to offer payback.

Standing back watching, Carmen caught the

tormenter in action. Apparently, this girl had found out that the boy she liked was actually interested in Jill, so she pestered Jill incessantly. This time, she made fun of Jill's clothes and her lack of a bust while emphasising her own designer clothes and well-developed figure.

Fittingly, Carmen produced a gust of wind to mess up the girl's hair, and she caused the girl's buttons to pop open. The bully squealed, not knowing what had happened, and ran to the girl's washroom to repair the damage. Jill, Carmen and all the onlookers, including the bully's friends, laughed at the hilarious scene.

That event and others certainly bonded the sisters.

Carmen phoned Peter to tell him of her plans, and she got the distinct impression that his feelings were hurt.

"You still want to meet my mother, right?" Peter asked.

"Of course. I'm looking forward to it. Don't worry, Peter, we are good," she reassured him.

"Can we get together tomorrow?"

"I'd love to see you tomorrow," Carmen heartily agreed.

With relief in his voice, he wished her a good night.

She hung up the phone, put on her walking shoes and headed out the door. Mrs. Roberts was outside watering the pots on her front steps next door. She looked up, put down her watering can and headed over to Carmen. Carmen had no idea what to expect and was a little afraid.

"Carmen, I'm so sorry," Mrs. Roberts said. "I had no idea what he was doing. I guess I didn't raise him as well as I thought I did."

"Oh, Mrs. Roberts, don't blame yourself. I think you are a great mother to Allan, and I had no idea either. Children don't always turn out the way that their parents want them to, and I certainly don't blame you."

"I've told Allan to give back all the things he took, and to pay to replace anything he couldn't return. He wasn't very happy with that idea, but I think he realizes it's the right thing to do. He will be going to jail, unfortunately, but that's how he'll learn his lesson. Hopefully he won't become worse by being there." Mrs. Roberts turned back to the house with her head down and finished watering her red geraniums.

Carmen ambled for several blocks before she found herself alone, and she lifted herself up to the rooftops of the taller buildings in her neighbourhood.

She sat contemplating for a while and watched the pedestrian traffic thin as the sky darkened. She observed a couple arguing in front of the shoe store, the man becoming increasingly loud and rough with the woman. He accused her of flirting with his friend, and although she denied it, he continued to shove her against the building.

Carmen interceded by having his fist hit the wall instead of her face.

He grasped his hand in pain, but this only made him more angry. He shoved the women again, but before Carmen could do more, the woman thrust her knee into his groin, hard. He fell back onto the sidewalk, clutching himself in agony.

The woman kicked him again and yelled that she

never wanted to see him again. Then she ran. The man was unable to follow her.

Carmen was quite impressed. Usually, abused women she had seen had been unable to separate themselves from their abusers. "Way to go, girl!" Carmen said to herself. "Payback's a bitch!"

She floated down and headed home to bed, appreciating that the people of the town didn't always need her.

5

O n Saturday evening, Carmen dolled herself
up, hoping to impress Peter's mom, and Peter
too. She donned a peacock-blue spaghetti-strap
dress with light-grey high-heeled sandals. She wore her
hair down but clipped back at the temples so she looked
somewhat innocent too. She carried a small clutch purse
that matched her shoes, and since it would be cool at
night, she wore a short, lacy crocheted sweater. Fine,
dangling gold earrings were the icing on the cake.

Peter arrived right on time, and his mouth dropped
open when he saw her. "Wow, you look beautiful."

He looked great too. He was wearing jeans with a
slightly shimmery slate-blue shirt under a black blazer.
He could wear a burlap bag and still look awesome,
Carmen thought. He was also wearing sunglasses, but
she could still see him eyeing her. *Mission accomplished!*
She smirked. All the trouble had definitely been worth
it. Now to win over his mother. Peter helped Carmen
into his car. *Well, his mother can't be too bad since*

she raised him into the remarkable man that he is, she thought.

While they drove to Peter's childhood home, he grasped her hand. He was sweating a little too. They reached the house in about twenty minutes.

On the driveway getting out of another car was a tall, white-haired man just the spitting image of Peter. *Wow,* Carmen thought, *Peter is* always *going to be a knockout.* The man looked up, waved and walked eagerly to Peter's side of the car to give Peter a typical man hug with the hard pats on the back. *No, you can't look sappy hugging another man,* Carmen mused sarcastically.

The man looked over the roof of the car to Carmen and said, "introduce me to the woman you find important enough to bring home for scrutiny." He laughed, and he and Peter walked around the car toward Carmen.

Peter put his arm around Carmen. "Uncle Joe, this is my girlfriend, Carmen. Carmen, this is my uncle, Joseph Anderson."

Mr. Anderson reached out both his hands, took Carmen's hand in one of his, and patted the top of it with his other hand. "I'm very pleased to meet you, Carmen! Welcome." He directed her to the front door of the house. "Peter's mother has been preparing all day to meet you. The house is spotless, as you women always feel is necessary, and if dinner tastes as good as it smells, we are in for a treat, and I should have put on looser pants." He laughed a hearty laugh that made Carmen feel very comfortable.

Peter opened the front door and guided Carmen inside

with a gentle hand on her back. The smell that greeted them was just heavenly. Carmen's stomach grumbled.

Peter commented on the smell, and his uncle said, "See? I told you it smelled great."

A lovely-looking woman came around the corner from the kitchen into the hallway, removing her apron as she walked. She was slender and had chestnut-coloured, jaggedly cut hair with highlights and lowlights. She was wearing skinny jeans and a pink-and-orange striped T-shirt.

Peter's mother was chic and appeared to be friendly. "Hi, sweetie," she said to Peter as she kissed him. "Hi, Joseph. And this must be Carmen." She gave Carmen a light hug. "It is so nice to meet you. Peter has talked about you occasionally over the years and it is about time you two got a little more serious!"

"Mom!" Peter yelped. "Don't embarrass me!"

"I'm sorry, dear, but a woman should always know how you feel, and it isn't as though she is completely blind to how you feel about her."

Then she whispered to Carmen, loud enough for Peter to hear, "I see the way he smiles when he talks about you."

"Mom!" Peter yelped again, and he led Carmen to the living room.

"By the way, since Peter forgot to introduce us properly," Peter's mother teased, "my name is Rachel, and you may call me that." She retied her apron.

"Well, Carmen, this will be a very short visit tonight," Peter teased right back.

"You can leave whenever you want." Rachel hesitated

for effect. "As long as you leave Carmen here." She licked her finger and signed the earning of a point in the air. "I'll check on dinner." Rachel tucked her hair behind her ears and walked back to the kitchen.

"Could I help you with anything?" Carmen offered.

"No, no, you are my guest," Rachel said. "Besides, it is just about ready anyway."

Dinner was as delicious as it smelled. Carmen tried not to overeat, but it was difficult. Uncle Joe had a good appetite; it was amazing that he stayed slim. But that's how it was with some people. Not with Carmen, though. She had to watch every mouthful.

The four of them had a great conversation over dinner. Uncle Joe wanted to hear all the gory details about working in a hospital, which was quite refreshing for Carmen because most people didn't. And Carmen loved to talk about her work.

"What is the grossest thing you have ever seen?" he asked

"You want me to tell you now, at the dinner table?" Carmen looked for everyone else's response.

Rachel scrunched up her nose.

"I'll tell you later," Carmen said to Uncle Joe.

The other diners then asked Carmen about her family, her life, and her work.

She gave just enough information and didn't go into the regrets, the disappointments, and her little secret. But at one point, she knocked over the gravy boat and supernaturally corrected it without realizing that she was using her powers. Uncle Joe seemed to notice and pulled a funny face, but then he just rubbed his eyes. Rachel and Peter had been looking at each other and missed it. Carmen just acted as if nothing strange had happened.

She wondered how Peter would react if he knew about her mystery. She wouldn't want to lose him like she had lost a dear boyfriend in college, who had called her a freak and left her.

They shared their family tales, and Rachel divulged some hilarious events in Peter's life. Carmen thought Peter's mother just might pull out the naked baby pictures at any time. *I have already seen your son naked*, Carmen thought, and she tried not to smirk.

She contemplated what the deal was with Joe and Rachel. He was the brother of her late husband, and sometimes relationships started with the brother caring for the widow. They seemed comfortable with each other, but there certainly wasn't anything romantic between them, at least not that she could see.

Peter was keeping cool too. Of course, you don't grope your girlfriend in front of your mother. Carmen liked them all, and she was having a very pleasant evening.

"Do you plan on having children, Carmen?" Rachel asked. Oh, there was the inevitable question mothers everywhere asked as they searched for the clues of whether the potential daughter-in-law was suitable.

Well, I guess I am suitable then. "Yes, Rachel, I would like to have children. I feel that they make life complete."

"Yes, they do." Rachel looked proudly at her son.

There came the brownie points! Carmen drank the last sip of her tea and placed the fine teacup back on its saucer. She fidgeted for a moment, aware that silence had fallen. She looked up and noticed everyone was off in dreamland. Rachel was most likely thinking about grandchildren, and Peter was possibly imagining making children. Carmen laughed. Everyone looked at her.

"What's so funny?" Peter asked, putting her more on the spot.

"Oh, nothing. I was just thinking." That might have made her appear rude. She had to think of something quickly. "Today I saw a boy who was laughing at his sister who had dropped her ice cream, so she knocked his out of his hands. It made me remember the old saying, 'I'll fix your wagon.'"

Everyone looked at her blankly.

"I guess you had to be there," she said.

"That's an old saying," Joe said. "I think it comes from the covered-wagon era. It doesn't refer to fixing the wagon in a positive way but rigging it to break down."

"I've never heard that one before, Uncle Joe, so it must be old," Peter kidded.

"Are you saying I'm old? You young whippersnapper!" Joe joked. "I didn't live in the times of covered wagons, you know. Anyway, I'd best be getting home so I can put my old self to bed." He pushed his teacup away and stood up. "Delicious meal as usual, Rachel. Thank you very much. Are we still on for bowling tomorrow afternoon?"

"Oh, yes. I'm looking forward to whooping your butt," Rachel challenged.

"Ha, in your dreams," Joe teased, and he headed to the front door. Rachel saw him out. "You take care of yourself now, dear. Lock the door behind me, and I'll see you tomorrow."

"Good night," Rachel said sweetly.

"Good night." Joe gave her a peck on the cheek.

Peter sneered. He probably didn't want things to go any further than companionship, out of respect to his father. "Let's clean up and then we should be going too."

"Okay, sweetie," Rachel said. "I'll take your help only because I don't want you to go yet." She appeared tired. She had no doubt worked hard today. The dinner had been a success.

After about fifteen minutes, Carmen yawned.

"That's enough. You two go home." Rachel nudged them out of the kitchen. "The rest can wait till morning."

Peter took Carmen home. He escorted her into her house, making sure all was safe and leaving with a kiss to keep her warm all night. He told her how much he would miss her while she was away at her sister's and that he hoped she would find what she needed there. "I'm here for you, too, Carmen. Don't forget that, okay?"

"Thanks, Peter. I just need a little time away, to refresh. Meeting your family was quite helpful as well. I won't be gone for more than a couple of days, and I can call you if you'd like. I'll even send texts occasionally."

"Yes, I'd like you to call me, and text. All right, you take care, and I will see when you get back. It will be a nice surprise for your sister." Peter kissed her again and left.

Carmen watched him leave and almost felt like cancelling her trip altogether. But they were getting close fast, and she needed to keep the other areas of her life going.

In the morning, she got ready for her trip, grabbed her suitcase and headed out. It was a beautiful day for a drive. It had rained lightly overnight, so everything smelled fresh, but the sun was now shining. She put the window halfway down as she backed out of her driveway.

Her neighbours Steven and Vanessa were playing on their front lawn. Steven seemed to be playing a little nicer this time. Vanessa waved at Carmen, so Carmen rewarded her with a butterfly landing on her sleeve. Vanessa squealed with delight. Carmen basked in the sweet sound of a child's joy, remembering Gautama Buddha's advice: "Do not overlook tiny good actions, thinking they are of no benefit; even tiny drops of water in the end will fill a huge vessel."

During her road trip, Carmen watched the people out for various reasons and tried to imagine what those reasons were. The people that were dressed up might be going to church. A man in a full pickup truck was probably going to the dump. A couple pulling a boat were going to the lake. Others, she imagined, were going to Grandma's or the shops, or the park.

A little girl in another car showed her stuffed kitten to Carmen through the window and waved. Carmen waved back and smiled, and treated the family in the car to a mother and baby deer at the side of the road. The little girl pointed excitedly at the deer, so her father slowed the car to get a better look. Carmen drove on, quite satisfied with herself.

Carmen turned her attention back to the road in front

of her. Then, in her rear-view mirror, she saw a motorcycle weaving between the cars, even the big trucks. He was driving much too fast and so carelessly. "You have a death wish," Carmen said.

He zoomed past her with a loud whine. Two cars ahead of Carmen's, the small Jetta was changing lanes. There was no way the motorcyclist could weave away, unless Carmen intervened. "If it *is* your day to die, Death will have to find you on another highway, not here, not now." She straightened the fingertips of both hands clinging to the steering wheel and sent a burst of her powers to the motorcyclist, lifting him up into the air, over the Jetta and into the space beside a Mini. She inhaled quickly and exhaled only when she saw that all was well on the road.

She thought of the damage that the motorcyclist could have caused and remembered the little girl with the kitten. *I can't let you get off that easily*, she thought. *You have to learn not to drive like an idiot.* So, after thinking a moment and seeing the motorcyclist a ways up the road, again acting careless, she scooped him up and sent him into the grass along the highway with just enough force to shock him into changing his ways.

She pulled her car to the shoulder along with some others and dialed 9-1-1. She went to the man to care for him until the ambulance and police came.

She made a sling for his broken arm with his shirt and lectured him, "You could have done some real damage, you know. You had better drive with more care from now on."

The rest of her drive was uneventful.

She reached her sister's house just before lunch. She

hoped Jill wouldn't see her until she actually came to the door. She walked quietly up the steps to Jill's Tudor-style home and rang the doorbell.

Jill came to the door drying her hands on a kitchen towel. Looking up, she gasped. "Carmen! What a surprise! I love it!" She hugged Carmen tightly and invited her in. "Gary, kids, look who's here!"

Gary came from the back of the house, and the kids scrambled down the stairs. "Aunt Carmen, Aunt Carmen!" the children echoed.

"Are you going to sleep over?" Jessica asked. "You can have my room if you want."

"That would be lovely, Jessica. Thank you. Does your room still have pretty yellow wallpaper with pink flowers?"

"Yes. The only thing that we changed were the curtains. They are frilly ones now."

"That sounds nice," Carmen replied.

"My room is changed," Bradley piped in. "Daddy painted a train on the wall. Come see, come see."

"Wait, kids, let Aunt Carmen get settled in first," Greg ordered as he took Carmen's suitcase.

"You look like you're running away from home again," Jill said. "Remember that time you took your doll and a couple cookies in a baggy and left on your bicycle?" She laughed.

"Which time?" Carmen asked, joining in the laughter. "There were many times, just different cookies. Always the same doll. But I always came back because of you."

"Well, the sight of me chasing you down the driveway screaming was probably very persuasive."

"It sure was," Carmen remembered.

Greg, Jill and the kids were planning to go to church in the evening, and Carmen didn't want them to change any of their plans for her. Besides, she hadn't been to church for a long time and thought it was about time she made restitution with her Maker for the way she judged others and took worldly events into her own hands.

They piled into the minivan, the kids shrieking with delight. They thought that perhaps church would not be so boring with their aunt along.

The kids fought to sit beside her in the van and in the church, so Carmen sat with one child on either side. She treated them with candies from her purse. Jessica laid her head on Carmen's shoulder while she sucked on her butterscotch. Bradley put his tiny soft hand in hers. Carmen was in heaven.

They sang the songs, Jessica with rather good tone, but Bradley almost screeched like a banshee. Carmen winced in pain at the high notes he bellowed but chuckled to herself at his eagerness to praise the Lord.

Carmen sang too. She remembered most of the songs from her childhood when her mother brought her to church to banish her abnormal ability. It brought back sad but also happy memories.

Carmen once had a Sunday school teacher, Mrs. Gibbons, that was quite fond of her and complimented her more than her mother ever had. She sometimes dreamed that the teacher was her mother instead. Of course, that was impossible. Mr. and Mrs. Gibbons were occasionally guests for dinner, and Mrs. Gibbons would tell Carmen's mother how pleased she was with Carmen.

It was time to stand to sing again, and Bradley pulled Carmen up and held the hymnal with her. He was such a sweet little boy. Carmen wanted so much to have a son just like him someday.

The sermon was from the book of Exodus. The preacher read: "But if there is any further injury, then you shall appoint as a penalty life for life, eye for eye, tooth for tooth, hand for hand, foot for foot, burn for burn, wound for wound, bruise for bruise."

Carmen found this all very interesting and even wondered if fate had brought her here today. Was she supposed to hear all this? This was already what she was doing. She believed in God, blessings and consequences but didn't really believe in hellfire. She knew God was the ultimate judge and that everyone would eventually get what was coming to them.

But eventually was a long time. She was giving people their what for, right now.

Was what she was doing acceptable? She certainly wasn't perfect herself. But she had this gift. She might as well use it.

Suddenly, Carmen heard Jessica softly snoring on her shoulder. *How nice. How about a sweet dream for a sweet girl? A dream about fairies. Yes, that's what I will give you.* She concentrated and watched Jessica smile while she slept. She felt pleasure herself from Jessica's dreaming. She thought about what Ma Jaya Sati Bhagavati said: "When you plant a seed of love, it is you that blossoms."

When church was over, the family headed home.

"What did you think about the sermon, Carmen?" Jill asked. "It was kind of fitting for you, eh? It made me remember that time our neighbour Danny Collins threw my doll in a mud puddle. You made a big dog come out of nowhere and chase him down the street."

Jessica looked at Carmen. "How did you make a dog come out of nowhere, Aunt Carmen?"

Carmen pulled a face at her sister for spilling the beans, and turning back to Jessica, tried to clarify. "Oh, Jessica, the dog just happened to come around the corner at the right moment."

"Was your dolly all right, Mom? Could you wash her?" Jessica asked with concern.

"Yes, sweetie. My mommy gave her a good bath in the washing machine." Jill giggled.

"I think karma is great," Greg said. "People should be penalized or rewarded for their actions. Don't you ever see someone doing something wrong that you would love to get them for or stop them? Like putting a twirling light on top of your car when you see a guy speeding? We love to watch the bad guy in movies get what he deserves. We even cheer for it."

"Yeah, I love it when the bad kid at school gets detention," Bradley added.

Now it was Carmen's turn. "All our actions have a result, or a consequence. But, kids, revenge is not a good thing. Confucius said, 'Before you begin on the journey of revenge, dig two graves.'"

"What does that mean?" Jessica asked.

"It means that you can hurt yourself physically and emotionally when you take revenge on someone else."

"What is re-venge?" Bradley inquired.

"Well, here we are guys. Home, sweet home," Greg interrupted. He had tolerated enough of the whole conversation. "Last one to the slow cooker is a rotten egg." He laughed as he got out of the car, so quickly that his coat got stuck in the door. The kids howled with laughter and raced to the front door. Jessica won, of course, because her legs were longer, but Bradley put his best effort into the contest. Without the key, they couldn't be the first ones in anyway.

Greg pushed both of the kids out of the way, unlocked the door, and ran all the way to the counter, where the slow cooker waited.

"You went in the house with your shoes on, Daddy!" Bradley scolded. "You need to be punished."

"Daddy can sweep the floor," Jill declared. "That is fair penance for what he did."

6

Peter moped around the house after a hard day at work. He waited anxiously for a call from Carmen. But there was not even a text.

Poor Shelley tangled herself in his legs trying to get some attention from him. She seemed to sense that something was wrong so she did silly things to cheer him up. She rolled onto her back, raised her legs in the air and moaned. She pushed her nose under a couch cushion and flipped it over. It worked. Peter laughed and gave her a good scratch on the back and kissed her forehead. "Good girl."

He finally plopped himself on the couch with a beer and searched for a movie that might make him forget about Carmen for a while. He found a disaster movie with great special effects. About ten minutes into it, his phoned finally chirped.

"Hi, handsome," the text stated.

He was so thrilled to hear from Carmen that he dropped the phone. By the time he picked it up, it chirped again.

"How are things on the other side of civilization?" Carmen's text read.

"Miserable," Peter responded. "How are you?"

"Good. Why are you miserable? Rough day at work?" Carmen added a smiley face.

"No, I just miss you!" Peter sent a sad face.

They texted for a long time, and then Carmen excused herself to put Jessica to bed. She had promised to read a bedtime story to her.

Peter reread all their texts and got up for another beer. He had disregarded the movie, so he shut off the TV. When he got to the fridge, he changed his mind about the beer and decided instead to take Shelley outside and then hit the sack.

Shelley was thrilled to go out and was certainly not willing to go back inside when Peter first wanted her to.

"Okay, girl. How about playing ball for a while?"

Hearing the word *ball*, Shelley ran to find her ball. Finally locating it in a bush, she brought it back to Peter, who threw it for her numerous times.

She stopped only to get a drink from the little pond in Peter's backyard. A fish came to the surface and distracted her, giving Peter the out he wanted. He headed back in the house, tidied the kitchen a little and called the dog back in for the night. Now that darkness had fallen, she was willing to obey.

Peter got ready for the night, and Shelley curled up beside him in his bed. Peter turned off the light and imagined Carmen reading to her niece. He smiled, thinking about what a great woman she was.

Finally, when Greg was at work and the kids were at school, Carmen and Jill had some quiet time alone. Jill had taken time off from her job as a researcher for a small publishing company to be with Carmen.

They grabbed a second cup of coffee and headed to the family room to catch up.

"I really needed to talk to you, Jill," Carmen said. "The robbery really made me angry, and my thoughts actually scared me. My punishments are usually just petty, but I really wanted to hurt the thief. It was all a little too close to home. The worst thing was that he took Grandma's jewellery. It was almost like he had taken her away again." She took a breath.

Jill had listened and nodded, allowing Carmen to vent. Now she had a chance to give her support. "I understand how you feel. And feeling as though he took Grandma away from you makes perfect sense. Plus, you've never really hurt anyone. Like you said, you only did petty things to people who probably warranted a whole lot more." She curled her legs under her on the couch and held her cup in both hands.

Carmen got the impression that Jill was willing to listen to whatever she had to say. "On the bright side, I'm really falling for Peter. I have butterflies in my stomach when I'm with him and knots when I'm not. I truly hope we have a future together. I'd like to have what you and Greg have.

"But I have a big secret that I am just not ready to

share with him. I want more time with him and a stronger bond before I drop the bomb. But the longer I take, the more it will hurt both him and me if he can't accept it." Carmen dropped her head and stared at the bottom of her coffee cup. She didn't even remember drinking it. "I don't know what to do."

"Carmen, in the past, you've not had good experiences when people knew what you were capable of, so of course you're afraid. Heck, even our own mother couldn't accept you. But that was her problem, not yours. I, on the other hand, have always looked up to you and found you to be extraordinary. You got me out of problems many times, with and without your gift. And, yes, I do believe it is a gift."

These words brought tears to Carmen's eyes. Her sister, her wonderful sister. Even after the way their parents had treated them, they were a great team of siblings.

"However," Jill continued, "I don't think you need to be in a hurry to tell him. Heck, you could go through life with him and never tell him. Who says you have to tell your man everything? I'm sure they don't tell us everything. As a matter of fact, I don't think we would want to know everything about them. But if he is indeed the one, then he would love you like I do even if he knew that you are a freak!" She laughed.

Carmen laughed too. She got up. "Let's go out."

Jill stood up too. "How about shopping? Momma needs a new pair of shoes!" They both laughed, nudging each other on their way to the kitchen with their empty coffee cups.

"Thanks, Jill. I hope I haven't been a pain to you or your family."

"A pain? Are you kidding? I love having you here, and so do they. Now let's go find some people who need to make amends. I haven't seen you in action for some time now." Jill put up both fists as if ready for a boxing match.

At the mall, they found plenty of people with a bit too much pride and greed. Carmen even saw sloth, gluttony, wrath, lust and envy. There were so many opportunities. But most weren't worthy of correction.

But when a woman with an arm full of shopping bags looked the two beautiful sisters up and down with disgust, Carmen just couldn't resist.

She increased the weight of the bags, causing the woman to bend to the floor, and made her perfectly straightened hair frizz out like she had been in a rainstorm.

Jill fell into hysterics. "Oh, how I have missed this! Did you see how she looked us over and scrunched her nose at us? I think she was emanating pride, greed, wrath *and* envy." She cupped her mouth with both hands to hide her laughter.

Carmen was glad to see her sister enjoying her antics. She felt supported again, a weight fell off her shoulders. "Okay, let's go find some more heathens. Turnabout is fair play."

After several days of visiting Jill and her family, Carmen said her goodbyes, tears and all. With her suitcase in the trunk and the pile of pictures that the kids had coloured for her on the seat beside her, she headed down the highway.

However sad she was to leave, she couldn't wait to see Peter and be back in her own home again.

She had talked to him every evening to keep things fresh with him. When they spoke the night before, he said that he would have lunch ready for her at his place, if she wanted. How nice it was to have someone to come home to. She put a CD in the car stereo and sang along as she drove, enjoying the scenery along the way. She had packed an iced tea in the cup holder beside her and sipped it to relieve the dryness in her throat from all the singing.

It was amazing that almost all songs were about love or breakups. *Love is such an important part of our lives*, Carmen thought. She occasionally played a song over again to listen to the words more carefully. New love was exciting, but old love was familiar and rewarding.

Suddenly lights and sirens came up behind her. *Oh, crap, was I speeding? No, I wasn't*, Carmen thought. *I wonder what's wrong. It must be me; there isn't anyone else around.*

Carmen pulled over to the side of the road and put both hands on the steering wheel where the officer could see them.

The officer swaggered toward her car, inspecting the rear, and then up to her window.

"Licence and registration," he said arrogantly.

Carmen decided not to say anything. He seemed like the type who wanted to do all the talking. Eventually, he would tell her what she had done. She would wait. She handed him the two documents.

He took them back to his car. He would find nothing outstanding, so he should be lenient about whatever this offence was, Carmen reasoned. He came back and handed her the documents.

She couldn't stand it any longer; he wasn't offering her any information. She wanted a chance to change his mind before he wrote a ticket. "What is it, Officer?" she asked.

"Your tail light's out," he said.

"Is that all?" She clucked. "Gee, I thought it was something serious." *Oops, that was a mistake.*

"You think it's funny? This *is* serious! Do you know how dangerous it is to drive with a tail light missing?"

"Well, I—"

He cut her off by bringing out the dreaded ticket pad and began filling in the ticket.

"Wait, Officer. I didn't know. I'll get it replaced as soon as I get home."

"You might not make it home."

"Well, a ticket won't make the light start working." *But I can make it work*, she thought. And she willed it to turn on.

"Are you sassing me, ma'am? I am an officer of the law, out here to protect you. I will give you a ticket, and then you will go to the nearest garage and have it replaced."

"You don't need to talk to me that way. I want to see this light for myself." Carmen moved to get out to show him that the light was working again.

"Uh, ma'am, stay in your car," the officer demanded, putting his hand on his gun.

"Oh, please. You don't need to threaten me with your gun!" Carmen tittered.

"I am not threatening you. You are threatening me."

"One-hundred-twenty-pound me is scaring two-hundred-pound you?" She laughed.

"I am not afraid of you." The officer was losing control of the situation.

Carmen opened the door, forcing the officer to step back, and proceeded to the back of her car. "Which tail light?" she asked, trying not to sound suspicious. "They are both working."

"The driver's side." The officer looked at the lights with wide eyes. "Well, it was out, and I've already written your ticket.

"How could it be out one minute and then on the next?" Carmen wanted out of this stupid situation, so she caused the Officer's stomach to rumble, and his eyes went wide again.

"Just take your ticket and go get the light checked," he said, quickly handing it to her.

"I'm not taking that. You are a fraud trying to reach a quota."

"I am not. Just take the ticket and contest it if you want." He took a deep breath and grabbed his belly.

"What's the matter?" Carmen asked brazenly.

He ran to the trees on the other side of the ditch, snuck behind a bush and dropped his pants.

"Not so arrogant now, are you?" Carmen got in her car and drove away, hexing his car with no working lights of any kind. *You get what you give.*

Carmen stopped at the gas station near her home to fill the tank at what seemed a reasonable price compared to what it had been lately. *Still too high*, she thought. She put the nozzle back in the holder and closed the gas tank cover. She paid for the gas and got back in the car.

She was tired and fed up with driving. *The last thing I want to do is make something to eat. I'm glad Peter invited me for lunch.*

She pulled into her driveway, retrieved her suitcase from the trunk and headed to the house, struggling not to drop anything. She caught movement in her peripheral vision and glanced next door to find Allan walking across his porch.

"What the heck?" she said. *What is he doing home? He should be in jail. Bail! The bugger got out on bail. Unbelievable. How unjust is this world!*

Rage filled Carmen's soul, and before she knew it, she had sent a forceful jolt across the lawn, knocking Allan off the porch, down the steps and onto the ground.

"Yeoww!" Allan screamed, grasping his ankle and lying curled on his side. His mother came running out in response.

That'll fix his flint! Carmen lost all control and choked him with her force.

"Allan, what's wrong?" his mother asked.

He couldn't answer; he couldn't breathe. His mother panicked. Carmen saw the fear in her face. *What am I doing? Get a grip*, she said to herself. She let go of Allan and braced herself on the porch railing.

Mrs. Roberts looked her way.

"I think I broke my ankle." He cried.

"What happened?" Mrs. Roberts asked, kneeling to inspect Allan's leg. She looked up. "Carmen!"

Carmen ignored her.

"I, I um, fell down the steps," Allan said. "I don't know how I lost my balance. It felt like I was pushed. Then I started choking."

Mrs. Roberts helped him up, and he hobbled to the steps to sit down.

"I'll call an ambulance," Mrs. Roberts said. "Wait here."

Carmen went into the house, disappointed with herself. She was a nurse. What had she done? Why had she lost it? She shook her head.

After lugging the suitcase upstairs, she called Peter to tell him that she was home. He said he was happy to hear from her.

"How was the drive home?" he asked.

"Uneventful, until I got home. Guess who's out on bail."

"No, way! What idiot judge did that?" Peter exclaimed.

"One that needs a lesson in justice," Carmen retorted. "Do you believe in karma?"

"You mean people getting back what they deserve?"

"Yes."

"I believe in consequence, but I don't believe that God strikes people with lightning every time they do something wrong. There would be no one left. Why do you ask?"

"Because I think that someone should be out here stopping the unfairness and corruption."

"Like who, Carmen? There just isn't anyone that can handle all of it. We have to do our best to be decent and accept the things we can't change. You know Beatrix Potter? She said 'Believe there is a great power silently working all things for good.' Are you still coming for lunch? I'd really like to see you."

"Yes, and I'd like to see you too."

"How would you like a nice walk on the beach?" Peter asked.

"That sounds great," Carmen responded. "That's a great place to blow off some steam."

"Would you like me to pick you up? I'm sure you are sick of driving."

"I'd like that." Carmen could feel herself relaxing already.

They were at the beach just an hour later, walking hand in hand and barefoot in the wet sand at the edge of the lake. The soft breeze blew through their hair and Shelley's fur. Carmen inhaled deeply and let out a long sigh. "Man, I needed this!"

"You're having a rough time of it, aren't you?" Peter remarked.

She looked Peter in the eye. "Seeing Allan at home was just the last indignation."

He stopped, faced her and put his hands on her elbows. "I feel for you, Carmen, I do, but sometimes you just have to accept things the way they are. Let it go. It isn't good for you to keep all this stress in you. I know it's hard to brush it off, and I'm not one to talk, but try, okay?" He hugged her. "Bad things happen to good people. That's just the way it is. Now, let's enjoy the beach." He kissed her nose and ran into the water, scooping it with his hands and splashing her.

Shelley barked and chased Peter into the water.

Carmen winced at the cold water in her face, but it was refreshing. *Peter is wise*, she thought, *and right too. He is such a decent guy. I had better not blow this. No more negativity.* She ran to avoid a second dousing of cold water, with Shelley running after her.

They continued the horseplay until they became tired. "How would you like a frozen yogurt?" Peter suggested.

"That sounds delicious," Carmen replied, and they headed to the little pavilion at the edge of the boardwalk.

"Do you want one, too, you wet, smelly dog?" Peter kidded. Shelley responded to his look and to his voice with a tail wagging that shook her whole behind and one sharp yip. "I'll take that as a yes. Not that you ever say no. And you're going to need a bath when we get home."

Shelley wiggled backwards.

"She doesn't like that word," Carmen said

"No, she hates the bath, and it takes forever for her to dry." Peter ordered regular cones for them and a doggy cone for Shelley.

"Ahh, you've been here before," Carmen said.

"Yeah, we come here a lot."

And with that, Shelley wolfed down her little yogurt cone.

"Now, how do you expect to enjoy it when you eat it so fast?" Carmen asked with a chuckle. "Oh, now you're just going to stare at ours, are you? Well, just go ahead and stare. Yours is gone, and no one likes a fat piggy." Carmen laughed and felt the stress melt away.

Shelley continued to watch every lick they made as

they walked to the bench under the pavilion. They sat for a while talking, and not another negative thought came up for Carmen.

That is, until she witnessed a teenage boy throw his candy bar wrapper on the beach. Carmen directed the wrapper to swirl upward and hit the boy in the face. He grabbed it and threw it down again. Carmen directed it to fly up again. The boy looked strangely at the wrapper and stuffed it in his pocket.

"How strange was that?" Peter said, scrunching his face.

"No one likes a litter bug," Carmen said. *That settled his hash.*

Peter still looked baffled.

7

Peter's mother had called him to come over and help her with some things, so Carmen went to sit with Ralph. It was still bright outside, and she could still feel the sun on her skin from their trip to the beach. *I never put on enough sunblock*, she thought as she touched her hot, tight face.

"You've been sitting in the sun for about a hundred years, haven't you, Ralph? But you don't have any wrinkles. Ha, but you *are* bleached. And what has the pigeon poop done for you, eh?" She laughed at her own silliness.

From her perch, she saw a couple of cars side by side in the lane beside the bank. A group of men got out of the cars and opened the trunks. They then gathered between the cars to inspect one of the trunks. One of the men pulled a hockey bag out, put it on the ground and unzipped it.

Carmen saw large guns inside the bag. *Oh no, this isn't good!* At first, she wasn't sure if this was an illegal sale or the preparation for a robbery.

The men moved more bags from one trunk to the other. *A sale,* she realized. She dialed 9-1-1 on her cell phone and told the dispatcher what she saw. "Yes, a gun sale, 324 Maple Street, beside the bank."

A bearded man who appeared to be the leader of the buyers pulled out an envelope and handed it to the grey-haired man who appeared to be the boss of the sellers, and he thumbed through the money it contained.

Carmen positioned herself for a better view. As the bearded man inspected a gun, Carmen rammed it into his face.

"Hey! What the hell?" He looked at the head seller. "That's not how you treat the guy with the money, asshole."

"What are you talking about? These are prime-quality guns," a skinny man said. Carmen laughed at his ignorance.

Blood trickled from the bearded man's nose, and he wiped it with the back of his hand. For the first time, Carmen tried to manipulate another person's body, and she caused the bearded man to kick the skinny man square in his groin. *It worked.* She surprised herself. *I am getting so much better at this.* Wanting to try more, she pushed one of the other men into yet another, and a brawl began.

"I guess you don't need me anymore." She laughed. "That really got you all going." She leaned on the gargoyle and enjoyed the show.

Soon, she heard police sirens. *You idiots,* she thought. *Turn those off.* So, she turned them off herself, but it was too late.

The men in the alley quickly dispersed into the two

cars and sped off. *Oh, come on. Do I have to do everything?* She flattened tires on both vehicles so the men couldn't drive and then locked all the doors so they couldn't get out. *Gee, no one is going to believe this.* "What a vantage point you have up here, Ralph."

When police pulled up, Carmen wished the perpetrators' trunks to open and the doors to unlock so the police could arrest the men. She could see their bewilderment.

The officers called for backup, ordered the men to lie on the ground and cuffed them. They all murmured about what had just happened.

A police van soon arrived, and the officers shoved the criminals through the back doors.

"Well, Officer Hamilton is off duty now." Carmen floated down from the roof on the other side of the bank and landed softly behind the Laundromat. She walked to the corner to watch the police cars drive away and the crowd of onlookers disperse. *So many people. Did anyone see me?* she wondered.

She walked the block home, deeply inhaling the cool evening air. A faint smell of skunk kept her from sitting on her porch, even though she could have changed the smell to something better, like apple pie.

She removed her shoes and sat on the couch. Her favourite TV show was on tonight. She would watch that. Feeling lonely, she said, "I should get a cat." She pulled the blanket up to her face in place of a furry cuddler.

In the morning, she woke with dread for her return to work. She looked at the squirrel on the windowsill and debated whether she should open the window at all. *As long as I don't forget to close it again,* she thought. She greeted her little morning visitor with a peanut reward and then purposefully relocked the window. She took a long, hot shower, but all too soon, Carmen needed to leave for her shift. She took her toast with her, as she was running late.

Peter was working today, too, so she looked forward to seeing him. When she arrived at the hospital, she sent him a text.

"Lunch?:

"Sure, hot stuff! Where?" he responded.

"Outside?"

"K. Text when you can go."

Carmen headed to the fourth floor feeling quite content. But then it all fell apart. When she got out of the elevator, nurses looked her way and scattered. In the locker room, she heard snickering. *What is going on?* she thought.

When she got to the nurses' station, of course, Tina was the one who spoke up. "Well, look who's back from her little holiday!"

"Hello, Carmen. Welcome back," Diana added.

"Hi, Diana. Thanks. Is there anything new around here?" Carmen picked up her assignment.

"Not really," Diana answered evasively. "Same old, same old."

"Nope, there's nothing exciting around here," Tina said. "How about with you, Carmen? Anything new?"

"No, just spent some time with my sister. The burglary really upset me. I got my grandmother's things back, though," Carmen replied, more to Diana than anyone else.

"That's great!" Diana declared. "I felt for you. I have a beautiful heirloom necklace from my grandmother that I would hate to lose."

Call bells rang, so all the nurses dispersed.

"Nothing new? Ha! That's not what I hear," Tina said to another nurse.

When Carmen came back from lunch with Peter, Tina just couldn't resist. "A little workplace romance. Isn't that sweet? It is usually highly frowned upon and quite risky, but it's still sweet." Her voice dripped with undertones, but what she said was just subtle enough to be hard to prove as harassment.

"Yes, it is nice to be *young* and in love," Carmen said.

"In love? Or maybe it's just another fling."

"Another?" Carmen balked. "What is that supposed to mean?"

"That I think you've done this before," Tina said with her hands on her hips.

Everyone at the nurses' station was now watching them.

"Well, I haven't had the privilege of being in love like this before, and anyway, it is none of your business." Carmen turned away. "Besides, I have work to do, and we're no longer in kindergarten." She walked down the hallway, trying to calm herself.

A minute later, after the fury had subsided, she teared up but then realized she had said that she was in love. *Yes, I am,* she thought, and the tears turned into a smile. *And*

I'm surprised with myself for not turning her into a toad. Well, maybe I'll just give her one wart.

Carmen took a minute to send Peter a text, including the scuttlebutt. Minutes later, he was on the fourth floor.

"Where is Carmen?" he asked at the nurses' station. "And who here has nothing better to do than gossip behind people's backs?"

Faces turned to Tina.

"I don't care about me, but I think you owe Carmen an apology," Peter said defensively to Tina.

"Hardly!" Tina walked away.

Peter soon found Carmen.

"I'm okay," she reassured him. "I'm almost used to being the punching bag." She chuckled.

"Well, you shouldn't have to be."

"It seems like nice people get abused but unpleasant people beat the rap," Carmen said as she pushed her medication cart back to the med room.

Peter followed her. "Well, she shouldn't get away with it. This warrants a formal complaint."

"Are you kidding? That would just make her behaviour worse," Carmen said.

"But she shouldn't get away with it." He emphasized again. He wasn't allowed in the med room, so he waited outside until she came out.

"You can't change people like her, Peter," Carmen said. She squirted sanitizer on her hands and rubbed them together briskly.

A patient interrupted them. "Nurse, could I get your help please?"

"Sure, Mrs. Chapman. I'm coming. I'll see you after work, Peter." Carmen wiped her hands on her pants and followed Mrs. Chapman.

Later, Carmen received a text from Peter offering to drive her home. She accepted.

On their way, traffic had stopped. It was difficult to see why with all the cars in the way, but eventually they noticed that a man had stopped the traffic to allow a mother duck and her ducklings to cross the road. It was cute, and people were cheering. The little endearing waddlers were quite the sight.

Carmen felt inspired, but she couldn't think of a suitable reward for the man. Then another pedestrian gave the man a pat on the back. Carmen was happy to see others doing her thing.

Traffic soon started moving again.

"It's nice to see people working together for a change, instead of honking or hollering at each other," Peter said.

"Have you ever stepped up and rewarded someone?" Carmen asked.

"Yes," Peter answered. "I left baseball tickets for someone at work once. He had gone out of his way for someone else."

"Wow! That was generous."

"He was a baseball fanatic." Peter shrugged off Carmen's compliment. He stopped the car at a stoplight and turned to look at her.

"What did he do when you gave him the tickets?" Carmen asked.

"Well, he never knew they were from me."

"Wow. Anonymous giving is the most honourable

type." Carmen was impressed. *He wasn't looking for the thanks or the pat on the back; he just wanted to make someone else happy. He is remarkable.*

"Sometimes it is just more fun to make the recipient wonder." The light changed to green, and Peter stepped on the accelerator.

Soon they reached Carmen's house, and Peter pulled into the driveway. He turned to her, clearly waiting for an invitation to come in.

"Are you coming in?" she inquired.

"I didn't want to seem presumptuous."

Carmen laughed. "It's okay. You may assume that I want you to come in, because I do."

"Hey, check out your neighbour." Peter pointed. "He's on crutches."

"Why isn't that guy in jail?" Carmen queried. "I don't get it. What does someone have to do to get a little fairness around here? Do I have to take things into my own hands?" Immediately, Carmen recognized she should not have said that.

Peter appeared puzzle. He looked at her with penetrating eyes. "Now, don't be doing anything that will get you into trouble," he preached. "I wonder why he's on crutches. Or did you already take things into your own hands?" He hooked his arm into hers, and they walked up to the house.

Carmen didn't answer.

"I was kidding!" Something flashed in his eyes that told Carmen he was now suspicious.

How could she let him get close without finding out that she was a supernatural being? The situation was bound to get uncomfortable, Carmen knew, but she still wanted to put any confrontation off.

"You're not telling me something," he said.

If he only knew, she thought.

Carmen unlocked the front door, and they went inside. "Do you want something to drink?"

"I'd love something cold and strong, thanks."

"Come look through my limited collection and see what you might like." Carmen got two glasses out of the cupboard and put them on the counter. "I'm going to change. I'll be right back down."

"You don't need to change a thing," Peter said coyly.

"Pardon?" Carmen asked, turning back. But she had heard him. She smiled.

"Nothing. I'm just mumbling to myself."

Carmen changed into yoga pants and a light pink T-shirt, both of which hugged her curves. When she came downstairs, Peter eyed those curves in admiration.

She scowled and then adding a little strut to her step. "What are you staring at?" she flirted.

"A very beautiful woman." He took her in his arms. He ran his fingers through her hair and then across her cheek and lifted her face to meet his.

She closed her eyes, focusing only on his touch. She moaned. When he kissed her neck, she whimpered and let herself collapse against his strong chest.

He tightened his grip, laid her on the couch and lowered himself onto her, all the while kissing her neck and stroking it with his tongue.

She tilted her head back to give him full access to her

skin. She grabbed his biceps in her hands, pulling him tight against her breasts. She knew he could feel the rise and fall of her chest against his, and she could tell that he could hardly control himself.

He reached down and grasping the bottom of her T-shirt. Carmen raised her arms willingly, and he lifted it over her head. She felt the throbbing inside her.

He tossed her shirt aside and stroked her sides lightly with his fingers, sending shivers through her.

She shook herself, feeling the goose bumps rise with his every stroke. She reached for his shirt and opened every button slowly, staring into his eyes the entire time. Then she tossed his shirt on the floor with hers. She stroked his lean body, watching the goose bumps rise on his skin too.

With a deep breath, Peter lifted Carmen and carried her to the bedroom.

Carmen lay awake beside Peter, who slept contentedly. She reviewed the events of the day, reciting Tina's words over and over and carrying on conversations in her head. She tossed and turned until Peter finally woke.

"Are you okay?" he asked.

"I can't sleep."

"What's keeping you awake? Is it what happened at work?"

"Yes. I'm rolling it over in my head, telling Tina off, even when she isn't here. It is driving me crazy." She sat up. "I think I'll get some milk." She got up and put her housecoat on.

After a few minutes, she came back to the bedroom, removed her housecoat, lifted the covers and crawled back into bed. He felt warm, so she cuddled up to him. She laid her head on his chest and took a deep breath, taking in his masculine scent. *If I can't sleep now, there is something seriously wrong with me.*

Carmen dragged herself out of bed. She just didn't want to face another day at work. Why couldn't she just lie with Peter all day? Where was Peter? She heard noises in the kitchen. Intrigued, she grabbed her housecoat and headed downstairs.

There he was in the kitchen having prepared tea, toast, eggs, and fruit. She exaggerated pinching her arm. "Nope, I'm not dreaming."

"Good morning! Sit down; it's still warm." He pulled a chair out for her and then sat down as well. They talked about their favourite foods while they ate.

Everything Peter had made was delicious. "Thank you, Peter. What a nice treat." Carmen smiled.

"It was my pleasure," he responded. "Are you okay with being driven to work today? Or do you want to go in separately?"

"That's a bit of a dilemma. Add fuel to the fire and just ignore the fuss? Or don't give them something to talk about?"

"Honestly, I think we should go in separately and let things die down," Peter suggested. "But I'll do whatever you want to do."

"Then again," Carmen said, "I don't think we should have to act a certain way just for them. Who's going to see us coming in together anyway?"

"Okay. We'll just be ourselves," Peter said finally.

She kissed him. "I'm going to shower and get ready, okay?"

"Sure," he said as she left the room.

Things seemed normal at work. No one made a big deal that Carmen and Peter had come in together. Most people didn't even look. Even when Peter kissed Carmen, people ignored them.

On the fourth floor, things felt a little odd, and the other nurses seemed to anticipate something. Tina wasn't there.

Diana stepped forward. "I'm sorry I didn't jump in and fix things yesterday. Tina intimidates me, but I should not have let her talk to you that way. Anyway, a few of us complained, and she has been suspended."

"Really?" Carmen said. "You mean there's justice for a change?"

"Yes, and teamwork too," Diana said. "See? Payback's a bitch!"

"And so is Tina." Carmen and Diana laughed together.

Carmen put together her assignment and went into

her nearest patient's room. She found a new patient who was small and looked very tired. "Good morning, Mrs. Gordon. I'm Carmen, and I'll be your nurse today. I will start by checking your blood pressure, and then I'll get your morning medications for you, okay?"

The old woman nodded slightly.

When Carmen finished with the medications, she set Mrs. Gordon up for her breakfast. She didn't think this worn-out woman would be able to feed herself. However, just as she was about to get a nurse's aide to feed the woman, a young woman came in the room.

"Hi," she said to Carmen before putting her purse down on the chair and removing her sweater. She rolled up her sleeves, ready to work. "I'm Lynn, Elisabeth's daughter. I'll feed and wash my mom."

"That would be terrific," Carmen declared. She appreciated when family members came in to care for their loved ones. It was a load off her, and the patients liked it too.

While Carmen prepared the medications for the patient in the next bed, she watched Lynn. She was gentle and loving with her mother. She fed her slowly and patiently, not rushing her like so many people did. Lynn closed the curtain between the two beds to wash Elisabeth, and then Carmen heard her singing gently as the water splashed. It was inspiring.

Lynn needed compensation. What could Carmen do for her? *I know: an extra dose of energy, and a happy home.*

Carmen focused on her gift and then turned her focus to her current patient. Charlotte Phillips was in the hospital after falling down the stairs. She had badly bruised her face, and she had broken her wrist trying to catch herself. "Do you need anything for pain, Mrs. Phillips?" Carmen offered.

"Oh, yes, dear, if I may. I think it is going to rain today. I feel achy all over."

"I think the forecast did say something about rain today," Carmen responded. "I can give you some acetaminophen, if you'd like." Carmen felt sorry for Charlotte and imagined this elderly woman's fall. Then she remembered Allan falling down the steps of his porch. A twinge of guilt ran through her. *But Charlotte isn't Allan. There is a difference. Allan robbed me, and I doubt Charlotte did anything like that. Her fall was just an accident.*

Another nurse stuck her head in the door. "Carmen, bed 461b would like a laxative, when you get a chance."

"Okay, thanks," Carmen answered. "Sorry, Mrs. Phillips I need to go."

"Okay, dear. I'll see you later. Thank you!" Charlotte called loudly as Carmen left the room.

Carmen's whole day was filled with little niceties. One patient gave her a chocolate; another gave her a dishcloth that she had knitted. She loved days like this, with chatty patients, kindness, and teamwork, plus no Tina. Even the dirty look she got from Betty at shift change couldn't ruin the rest of her day. Maybe Betty was just ready for another rash.

She left work with her head held high, but at the entrance to the hospital, Carmen saw Lisa talking to a man. *Oh no. Don't fall for another one,* she thought, but something about the conversation didn't seem too friendly.

Lisa waved Carmen over. "Carmen, this is the lowlife that cheated on me, and now he wants me back. Isn't that just a scream?"

"Maybe you should just cut your losses and move on," Carmen said to the man. "Lisa can do much better."

"Stay out of it," the man said right into Carmen's face.

"Not after what I saw you do to Lisa."

He took a step back, surprised at Carmen's response.

"I'm done with you, Barry," Lisa piped in.

Barry opened his mouth to say something, but Carmen stopped him. "She says she's done with you."

"Yup. I don't stay with cheaters," Lisa said more confidently.

"Well, I wouldn't have cheated if you had kept me satisfied," Barry said as he spun around to leave.

Lisa's mouth gaped, but before she could say anything, Carmen said, "It isn't worth it. Act like you don't care." And with only a thought, Carmen gave Barry an uncomfortable case of tinea cruris, or jock itch, and an embarrassing trip off the curb.

Later, at home, Carmen got a phone call from her mother. It had been months since they had spoken. Hearing from her now made Carmen wonder what she wanted. Carmen answered.

"Hello, Carmen. It is your mother."

So formal, Carmen thought. "Hello, mother. How are you?" She resisted calling her ma'am, or Norma, but she chuckled at the idea.

Ignoring Carmen's question, Norma said, "Carmen, your cousin Alexander died on Sunday. I thought you should know. Your aunt Geraldine is taking it hard, so I would like you to send a sympathy card, and if you can, I think an appearance would be in good standing. The funeral is the day after tomorrow. You'll have to find a hotel room. I have other people already staying here at the house."

"I'm sorry to hear that. What happened?"

"No need to be sorry. You didn't do it. An intoxicated driver killed Alexander. There are still idiots no matter how often they tell them not to drive after drinking. I expect to see you at the funeral."

"Mom, I can't get off work," Carmen responded. "I just had time off to visit with Jill. There is no way they will let me take more."

"Well, this is important. If you can go off gallivanting with your sister, then you can take time for a funeral. That hospital should be more accommodating. Goodbye."

"Oh, take a flying leap," Carmen said to the dial tone. "I'm fine; thanks for asking, Mom. And yes, I love you too. Pfft." *I'm not going! I could send a card, though.* She found herself heading to the fridge. "No! I am not sabotaging myself because of her. Just forget she even called." Instead of having a snack, she poured a glass of lemonade and took it outside to the porch.

A couple of sparrows splashing in the birdbath made Carmen smile. But the tears followed close behind. She longed to have a supportive mother. *Like Peter's.* One she could talk to, shop with, tell her problems to, and go to funerals with. Then she remembered her grandmother. Now the tears came fiercely.

She pictured her tall, strong-spirited grandmother,

who reminded her of Glinda, the good witch from the *Wizard of Oz*. She missed her terribly. *Why did the good witch die and the wicked witch live?* She stopped herself from thinking so cruelly.

She took her empty glass back in the house. She noticed her cell phone light flashing.

"At Mom's tonight. How are you?" the text from Peter read.

"Just talked to my mom. Going to have a bath and drown my sorrows."

"Uh-oh. What did she say?"

"My cousin died; she wants me at the funeral. I'm not going. I can't take more time off work."

"Are you going to be ok? I can come over after I help my mom."

"No, you help your mom. The bath will do me good. Later."

So Carmen did have the bath. She took a book and a large glass of wine with her. She lit the candles around the tub, put lavender salts in and ran the water plenty hot. Soon the room steamed up. She let her clothing drop to the floor and put a toe in. Then she lowered herself into Eden and sighed deeply.

Once immersed in the fragrant water, she rubbed her arms and then her legs to soothe her skin. She remembered Peter's hands on her. She closed her eyes and pretended these were his hands caressing her.

She took a sip of merlot; it was bitter and tingled down her throat. After a second sip, she put the glass back on the ledge. She reached for her book and read until she felt waterlogged.

While Carmen was drying off, the phone rang again. "Gee, no peace around here," she said aloud. It was Sergeant Campbell.

"We retrieved more of your property, Carmen," he said right off the bat.

"That's great."

"We will let you know when you may have it returned to you. I am so happy for you. It doesn't always turn out this way."

"I guess I'm lucky."

"That isn't all. Since we had more evidence against Allan Roberts and the dollar value climbed, his bail has been revoked and he has been returned to jail."

Carmen was elated. "Thank you so much for calling, Sergeant Campbell."

She just had to tell Peter, so she called him. "I'm sorry to interrupt your visit with your mom, but I had to tell you my news." She filled him in on the details.

"That's awesome!" he said. "Now open your front door."

"What, why?"

"Just do it."

She opened the door, and there he was. "Peter! But, I—"

"Surprise!" he said with a big grin. "I was already on my way here when you called. I finished helping her clean her eaves troughs and headed over."

"You are a good son and a great boyfriend!" She hugged him.

"So, how did they find your things?" Peter asked, following Carmen into the house.

"There was a drug raid at one of his friend's places, and my stuff was there piled up in a corner."

"And so because of this, Roberts goes back to jail?"

"Yup. Karma is like a rubber band: you can only stretch it so far before it snaps back at you."

8

That night, Carmen dreamt about Allan Roberts: He sat on the bunk in his prison cell. Grey block walls surrounded him behind old metal bars crusted with layer upon layer of old paint, light grey over dark grey over medium grey. Chips of paint fell to the floor with just a touch.

A cold toilet, shared with a companion of questionable hygiene, sat in the open in the corner of the cell, where no privacy was offered.

Man, this place stinks! he thought. *I thought I had avoided this crap hole.* His foot throbbed. His head hurt. He lay down on the top bunk. *Damn squealing traitors. I gave them that stuff dirt cheap, and then they go and rat me out.*

Then that judge, sittin' all high and mighty, with her I-told-you-so attitude. Well, piss off, all of you! I never get no damned break.

He fumed over the day's events. But still he couldn't see how he had done this all to himself. *Why did that stupid Carmen have to leave her window open?* "Shouldn't tempt a guy like that."

"Shut up, dirt bag," his roommate said, kicking the underside of the mattress.

Allan reached under his pillow and pulled out the novel he had found in the prison's library, Bram Stoker's *Dracula*. "This should be good. Bite those losers!" He felt another kick from below.

"I said shut up. And if I have to say it again, I'll shut it for ya!" the con on the lower bunk raged.

"You shut up, shithead!" Allan yelled back. But he soon wished he hadn't. Short-fused Larry jumped to the floor and reached up to the top bunk. He grabbed Allan by the scruff, pulled him to the concrete floor and beat him.

The guards took their time coming to break up the fight. They didn't care. They actually got a good laugh out of inmates' fights.

By the time they pulled Larry off Allan, Allan was bloody, bruised and unconscious.

"Aww, Larry. Why can't you play nice?" One of the guards laughed as he dragged Allan out of the cell. "Every time we give you a new playmate, we have to take him away again."

Tina was back from her one-week suspension. She stomped as she walked, glared at the other nurses and barely spoke. When she finally did speak, she started at Carmen again.

"Patient in 475's call bell has been ringing for fifteen minutes, you know."

"Oh, you have time to watch my call bells but can't answer any of them while I'm busy?" Carmen responded.

"I have my own patients to watch," Tina said defensively.

"Well, then, keep your comments to yourself."

"Take better care of your patients and I will," Tina argued.

Carmen had had enough. "Your suspension didn't teach you anything, did it? We are supposed to be a team here." Almost without contemplation, Carmen delivered a booming headache to the wicked woman. *And a little alopecia appearing overnight might keep you home for a while,* Carmen thought.

Another nurse stepped up. "Tina, you have got to stop. Why are you so nasty? If you hate being here so much, why don't you retire?"

Other nurses agreed.

Tina clenched her temples. "You all gave me a migraine!"

"No, actually, that was just me," Carmen admitted.

Everyone looked puzzled, but they scattered when they saw the manager coming down the hall.

Carmen slipped into the ladies' room and splashed water on her face to calm herself. She tried to stay away from Tina for the rest of the day.

Carmen dragged her feet on the way home. Tired and discouraged, she wished for peace in her life. She had never really had any at all.

She stopped in the little pet shop on her way home. It was amazing that it was still here, with big-box stores taking business from so many smaller ones. But this store had mom-and-pop service.

The variety of animals made the store popular, too. Animals always cheered Carmen up. She watched the kittens tumbling with each other and the puppies biting each other. A hamster ran around and around on its wheel. *I feel like I'm going around and around but getting nowhere, too. No matter how I intercede, there is still more wrong to stop.*

Lara McCraken, an old friend of Carmen's, happened in.

"Carmen! How long has it been?" Lara had long, brilliantly red curly hair reaching halfway down her back, just like she had in high school. She had it pulled back with barrettes to keep it out of her face. She was slender except for a perfectly round belly protruding under her tight yellow jersey shirt. She held her belly with one hand and her oversized handbag with the other.

"It's been a long time," Carmen answered. "How are you?"

"I'm great." Lara rubbed her belly. "I'm pregnant!"

"That's great," Carmen replied, not needing the verbal information. She was a little reluctant to answer because it wasn't always great to be pregnant, but Lara sounded happy, so it must be great.

"I married Steven Loomis from high school. Remember Steven?"

"Yes, the brainer in math class," Carmen recalled.

"Yes, that's him," Lara said proudly.

They talked for a while to catch up. "Would you like to meet up one day for coffee or something?" Carmen asked.

"How would you like to help me with a little baby shopping?"

"That sounds like fun," Carmen answered. They agreed to meet sometime soon, and then Lara bought some dog bones and left the store.

She's done well with her life. Sure, fate, rub it in my wounds, why don't ya? Carmen thought.

She continued her walk home, and a bicyclist on the sidewalk knocked her off her footing. She gave him a flat tire. A pushy person in a car honking got an overheated engine. And a man who didn't hold the door for the woman with two kids walking behind him shaped his own future of an earache.

This is fun. Carmen giggled to herself while she helped the woman and her kids. "Hey, buddy, next time try to be a little considerate of people who are behind you."

One of the children looked at Carmen. "You're Wonder Woman, aren't you? Where's your costume?"

"It is at the cleaners." Carmen laughed and rubbed the child's head, knowing the child had sensed her power. Carmen walked the rest of the way home with a skip in her step.

Peter picked Carmen up, and they met his mother at a restaurant. Carmen appreciated that Peter was always punctual.

Carmen and Peter had arranged to meet with his

mother for lunch. They had chosen a little restaurant near Town Hall called Europa Bistro because it advertised a special that sounded delicious. Rachel hadn't been there, but Peter and Carmen both had

"I hope eating here doesn't remind you of some old boyfriend," Peter teased.

"It won't," Carmen replied. "To prevent such memories, you would be safe with anyplace except Burger Buddies." She laughed.

"Well, I was going to take you there next time." He smiled.

"Good, then you can erase the memory I have of that place."

Peter had offered to treat, but his mother would have nothing to do with it. "I am the oldest, so I pay."

"Since when is that the rule?" Peter asked.

"Since I made it," Rachel said.

"Well, my rule is that the man pays," Peter insisted.

"That's sexist," Rachel said, and with that, she won the debate. She patted her son's cheek.

Rachel's outfit was just as classy as the one she wore the first time Carmen saw her. This time she wore black skinny dress pants with flared legs and a fuchsia silk blouse, with lipstick to match. A long bulky necklace tinkled delicately when she moved.

Peter had donned black corduroy pants with a purple-and-green paisley dress shirt, and he looked as handsome as ever. He must have put something in his hair because his curls were more defined. Carmen liked it.

Carmen wore a red dress with a low back and high

neckline, and no necklace at all. She stood on pumps of the same colour. It was simple but chic. Gold earrings hung almost long enough to touch her neck. Three fine gold bangles adorned her wrist.

The restaurant was warm and cozy, with thick, plush carpeting; walls plastered with scallops; and a chandelier over each table. The dishes were brightly coloured earthenware and the cloth napkins were a bold orange. Dense palms divided each table into its own private oasis.

Everyone ordered the special for lunch. Rachel ordered white wine, Peter ordered beer and Carmen requested ice water with lemon.

"Go ahead and order something to drink," Rachel insisted.

"No, really, this is what I prefer with my meal," Carmen assured her.

"Okay, but if we get a buzz and you don't, you might think we act strange." Rachel laughed.

"I'll try not to be a drag." Carmen laughed as well.

Carmen liked that Rachel treated the restaurant staff like friends and equals and not like hired help the way some people did. She could see where Peter got his people skills.

"So, Carmen, what department do you work in?" Rachel asked.

"I'm in frontline nursing on a medical floor," Carmen answered.

"That must be very rewarding." Rachel laid the napkin on her lap.

"Yes, it *is* very rewarding. I enjoy it very much."

"Which one of you two has worked at the hospital longer?"

"I've been there for fifteen years," Peter said.

"I've been there for eleven," Carmen answered, and she took a sip of her ice water.

"And you waited this long to start seeing each other?" Rachel asked rhetorically.

But Peter answered, "When I first met Carmen, she was seeing someone. Then I was seeing someone. We didn't think dating coworkers was a good idea. But now here we are. After getting to know each other as coworkers and friends, we're …" He hesitated, looking at Carmen. "Dating."

Carmen was afraid he would say lovers. She was relieved that he didn't.

"Well, I think you make a cute couple," Rachel said. "Now, would anyone like dessert?"

"Not me. Thank you, Rachel," Carmen answered.

"You keep a lovely figure, Carmen. It is hard to resist at times, though, isn't it?" said Rachel.

"Yes, and you look like you take good care of yourself as well."

"You are beautiful women," Peter said. "I feel privileged to be sitting here with you both."

"I taught him well, didn't I, Carmen?" Rachel laughed. "'Always compliment a lady,' I said."

"Yes, you taught him many things well, Rachel," Carmen said. "He has impeccable manners and treats me well."

"Well, he had better!" Rachel joked. "But seriously, he

learned a lot from his father too. He was a terrific man. He has been gone six years now, and I miss him dearly."

"I'm sorry," Carmen said sincerely, and she granted Rachel a little comfort in her heart.

"Well, let's not get gloomy now. Where is that dessert menu?" Peter interjected.

"You think you're going to eat dessert in front of two women who try to resist?" Rachel scolded her son.

"I work hard; I can burn it off," he replied.

"Hey, we work hard too, you know," Rachel reminded him. "No dessert for you."

Peter scowled like a little boy. Carmen laughed. *I love that man*, she thought.

Peter took the napkin off his lap, scrunched it up and placed it on the table. "Well, let's go then, if there's no dessert." He pushed his chair back.

The women got up too. Rachel left money on the table.

Peter was very attentive to his mother, helping her get up, guiding her from the table.

Carmen knew that men who treated their mothers well usually treated their women well. *As long as they didn't put their mothers before their wives. No one likes a momma's boy.*

"Where do you live, Carmen?" Rachel inquired.

"On Blossom Avenue."

"Can we show my mom your place?" Peter asked. "Carmen has made a lovely home, Mom."

"Uh, yeah, um, sure. If you want to," Carmen babbled, thinking it a little too early for this.

"I'd love to see your place. Is it a house or an apartment?" Rachel asked.

"It's a house," Carmen told her.

"Come on. We'll show you." Peter said, waving toward their cars.

Soon, Peter pulled his car into Carmen's driveway, and Rachel pulled in beside his. They all got out, and Rachel looked around.

"What a lovely house, Carmen! And your yard is beautiful. Do you do your own gardening?"

"Yes, I love to get my hands in the soil."

"Me too! Maybe we can swap perennials sometime. I have some that are getting too big. Peter can show off his muscles and dig them up for us."

"Gee, thanks for volunteering my services, Mom," Peter said sarcastically.

"You're welcome, son." Rachel laughed. "It'll keep you in good shape. I've seen how Carmen looks at you."

Carmen's face went hot. She was mortified.

"Mom! Please don't embarrass Carmen," Peter cried. "It's okay, Carmen. My mom is just being silly." He touched Carmen's arm and scowled at his mother. "Let's show my juvenile mother your home."

Carmen was stunned at the way Peter stuck up for her to his mother. *Good. We have no momma's boy here.*

"I'm sorry, Carmen," Rachel said. "That was inappropriate of me. I was trying to tease Peter, but I embarrassed you instead. Please forgive me."

"Apology accepted," Carmen said.

As they stepped into the foyer, Rachel said, "Oh,

Carmen, you have done an exquisite job with your home." This wasn't a huge house, but it was big enough for a family and decorated tastefully with enough plants and leather and unique wall art made of metals and coloured glass fragments to make the place cozy. The hardwood floors gleamed. Soft neutrals covered the walls, and Carmen had modernized the kitchen.

"I told you she had similar taste to me," Peter said.

"Yes, you're right," Rachel said.

They spent an hour talking in the great room with tea, but then Rachel excused herself to go home. Peter seemed glad.

After Rachel left, Carmen told Peter that she liked his mom.

"Even though she embarrassed you?" Peter asked.

"Yes, even though she notices that I check out your bod," Carmen revealed.

"I check out your bod, too, Carmen." Peter put his arms around her and kissed her.

9

At Carmen's next shift, she had an entirely new assignment since she had been off for a day. It was always tricky to get to know five new patients and their sometimes multiple diagnoses. She got report from the night nurse and then went through the care plans, jotting down notes, and then she proceeded to meet the patients and get their medications.

Today, she was in for a shock. One of the patients on her list was Allan Roberts. "Do you mean *the* Allan Roberts?" she asked the night nurse.

"He's a con with guards by his bed," the night nurse said.

"Yes, that is *the* Allan Roberts. He's the one who burglarized my house. That's a conflict of interest. I'll ask the charge nurse to reassign him to someone else," Carmen said. "What is he doing in the hospital? Couldn't they take care of him at the prison infirmary?"

"I guess not," the night nurse answered. "Apparently a lot of the staff are absent with the flu."

Carmen peeked at him once as she walked by his room. He looked so pathetic curled up in the bed, facing away from her. She was glad that he didn't see her.

She managed to get through most of the morning without having to see Allan, but when he headed to the shower room near the nurses' station, they almost bumped into each other in the hallway.

"Watch it!" one of the guards said, grabbing the inmate's arm.

"Sorry," Allan said. Then, realizing who she was, he stopped and sincerely told Carmen that he was sorry for stealing her things. "It was stupid of me. I know there is no excuse, but I am getting counselling and trying to be a better person. You were always nice to me, and I should have told my buddies to forget it when they came up with the idea of stealing your stuff. Again, I am really sorry."

Carmen was so surprised that she didn't know what to say. "I … I …" Was all she could manage. Allan wore an orange jumpsuit and handcuffs. He was covered with cuts and bruises, Steri-Strips and bandages. He had a fat lip and was a real mess. The cast was still on his leg, and he had an IV in his arm. Her dream had been real; his cellmate had beat him badly.

"Come on, get to the shower!" the guard interrupted, pushing Allan along. "No one wants to hear the apology of a scumbag."

Carmen stood stunned. *How humiliating for him*, she thought.

Diana came by. "Wow, do you think he really meant it? I mean, he sounded genuine."

"I don't know what to think," Carmen admitted, and she returned to the nurses' station.

After lunch, Allan's mother came in with some flowers. "Carmen, these are for you. Allan phoned me and asked me to bring them as a gesture of good will from him."

Carmen was stunned again. "Thank you, Mrs. Roberts. I'm sorry that all this happened, and for what it did to you as well."

Later, an hour before her shift was to begin, Lisa was on the unit working.

"Lisa, what are you doing here so early?" Carmen asked.

"I remembered there was something I forgot to chart yesterday and thought I'd better come in and do it. Plus, I wanted to have a chance to visit with Mr. Baxter for a while before I had to work. He is a lonely man."

"You are a good nurse, Lisa. May God bless you for your efforts." *In the meantime, I'll give you some extra stamina. I'm also going to enter your name for the nursing awards.*

Carmen's shift finished without any more interactions with Allan or his mother. She took her flowers home, pleased with Allan's gesture. Now she felt even more guilty for breaking his ankle and choking him.

On top of the bank that night, Carmen picked at the little stones and tossed them into the alley, where a considerable amount more action had taken place not long ago.

"Well, I don't know, Ralph. It's rather quiet tonight. Not much going on." Carmen patted the gargoyle's hard head. "Gee, speaking of quiet." She laughed.

I know! Let's do some testing, Carmen thought, so she made it appear that a twenty-dollar bill had fallen from a woman's purse. To her pleasure, the man behind her picked it up and returned it to her.

"Good man!" Carmen said. "Here, have some happiness."

She tried it again. This time, the young woman picked the money up, looked around and stuck it in her pocket. "You are a bad girl!" Carmen said. "Here, have a long dose of the hiccups!"

Another person insisted that he didn't drop the money when someone picked it up and offered it to him.

Carmen sat for a while watching the sun lower in the sky and then packed it in for the night.

When she got home, she did some laundry and paid some bills online, and just as she went to sit down, there was a knock on the door. Opening the door, she saw an older man there.

He was probably in his seventies, white hair, bald on top. He had a beer belly, was bow-legged and held a cane in his hand. He had a large red nose that indicated that he had been a drinker, but he had a sparkle in his eyes.

"Carmen?" he asked. "Is that you?" He smiled half-heartedly, apparently unsure of how she would react.

"Yes. Who are you?" Then Carmen looked carefully into his eyes. "Dad? What are you doing here?"

"Hello, sweetie." His eyes filled with tears. "You are beautiful! Truly, you are a sight for sore eyes."

Carmen just stood there astonished. She did not know what to think.

It had been so long. She hadn't known where he was, why he left or if he even cared. All her mother had done was speak ill of him. But then, she talked badly about everyone. "How did you know where to find me? Where have you been all these years? You left us! I have hated you all this time, and now you just show up out of the blue."

He tilted his head, tears still filling his eyes. When the first tear ran down his cheek, Carmen lost control, and her tears came too.

"I'm sorry. Let me explain." He stepped forward, reaching for her.

She stepped toward him, accepting his affection.

"My little girl." Carmen's long estranged father pulled her close and hugged her. "I'm sorry. I should have never let her keep me from you."

"What? Who?" Carmen asked, pulling back to look at him.

"Your mother," he answered.

"My mother? But why?" She took a step back. "Why would any woman keep her children from their father? That would be selfish and cruel." Her voice increased in volume and then cracked with emotion. "I needed you."

He wiped a tear from her cheek. "She made my life miserable, and eventually she told me to stay away from you. She even threatened me. It just became easier to do what she said."

"Come inside," she said, showing him in.

He looked around. "This is similar to the house you grew up in. Our house."

They sat for hours catching up. His life had been

miserable. He was lonely and had started drinking. He had searched for her before and had even begged Norma for their daughters' phone numbers, but she had refused to give them to him. Norma had never told Carmen. This made Carmen angry.

He hadn't wanted to go. Carmen could feel he was sincere. She knew what her mother was like, but the pain of having missed him for so long was heavy.

Carmen had ignored her phone for a couple of hours, but then finally picked it up when a call from Peter came through.

"Carmen, I've been so worried. Where are you?"

"I'm at home ... with my father."

"What? You're with your father?"

"I'm at *my* home with *my* father." She laughed when she realized how good that sounded.

"Your father came to your house after all this time? Are you okay?" Peter asked, concerned.

"I'm great," Carmen said. "I feel like a big hole in my life has been filled."

"Okay, you two have a nice visit. I'll see you tomorrow." He hung up quickly.

Carmen put down the phone. Her father left shortly afterward, and they had agreed to keep in touch. She decided not to call Peter back because she just wanted to revel in her thoughts. She finally understood something about what had happened with her father.

She was surprised but relieved that she had forgiven him and accepted him back into her life. She was happy that he had looked for her, and happy to know his side of the story.

She looked forward to seeing him again. Wow, would her mother be mad. *I should call her and tell her right now. Nah, I don't want to talk to her.*

The next day, there was a new plant sitting on the table in the nurses' lounge, and because of Diana's short stature, the plant almost hid her. Carmen inspected the card that came with it to see whom it was from. It was addressed to all the nurses from Mrs. Hofstadter, who had been discharged the day before.

"She mentions you in the card, Carmen," Diana said, pointing. "She was very fond of you."

"She was one of the unforgettable ones," Carmen replied.

"She noticed that you went out of your way for her," Diana added.

"I enjoyed taking care of her." Carmen sat down beside her coworker and friend. "Guess who knocked on my door last night?" she began when the other staff had left the room.

"Well, it couldn't have been Peter. I'm sure he doesn't knock anymore." She laughed, but then stopped when she saw how serious Carmen was. "Sorry, who?"

"My father."

"What? Your long-lost father?" Diana put her coffee cup on the table and turned her body to face Carmen.

"Yes. He wants to get to know me again."

"He actually came back after all these years?" Diana asked. "Do you think he's legit? Maybe he needs a kidney."

"Can't you accept that he just maybe wanted to reconnect with me?" Carmen suggested.

"I don't know. People are strange. Gee, who makes such a mess of our lunchroom all the time?" Diana said, changing the subject.

"There are a couple of people around here who don't clean up after themselves," Carmen said. "I guess their mothers didn't teach them very well." She chuckled.

"Maybe they think their mothers work here. Well, I am sick of sitting in their mess." Diana groaned.

That afternoon, Peter came up to have lunch. Carmen felt that he was trying to be supportive of her relationship with her father but that he was suspicious. He didn't push the issue with Carmen.

"How nice it would be for you if he truly were on the level," he said.

The fact that Peter and Diana had the same thought about Carmen's father made her uneasy. Was she being gullible?

Carmen filled him in a little about their visit. Then she told him about seeing Allan on her floor. She had so much to say, but it was soon time to go back to work.

"Half an hour is never enough for lunch," she said. She kissed him, and he asked if she wanted to play mini-golf after work. She said yes.

Back on the floor, Carmen noticed one of the aides sitting down on the job again. She wasn't a very hard worker, and lately her work ethic had gotten worse. She didn't seem to be depressed or in pain; she just didn't work very hard, and she sometimes told other people what to do. *That is enough of that*, Carmen thought. *Some hemorrhoids will keep you from sitting so much.* The aide jumped up rather quickly, as if something had bitten her. The look on her face was priceless.

"I'm so nasty," Carmen said.

"Why, what did you do?" Diana inquired.

"I just lit a fire under someone's butt, that's all," Carmen admitted.

Diana looked around in confusion.

"You know that these charts are supposed to go there, right?" Betty said to Carmen, pointing. She demonstrated how to tag a chart. "And I do this, like this."

"That's funny. Yesterday you told me they were supposed to go here." Carmen put the chart back in its original position. "Do you change the rules depending on the day, or just to have something to bug me about? You also give me heck for doing things the same way that everyone else around here does them. I'm tired of it. Leave me alone."

To Carmen's surprise, Betty walked away.

10

Mini-putt was a welcome distraction from the day. Carmen was delighted when it was time to go. It had been a favourite pastime of hers in her teens. She had played at this actual course back then, usually with Jill. The course had aged quite a bit, but it would be fun playing on the same holes just the same.

"Have you played much mini-golf?" Peter asked Carmen.

"I've played some but not a whole lot. You?" Déjà vu came over her. She had been here with a boy before, but she couldn't remember whom. She remembered losing on purpose to make him feel superior. *How dumb was that?* she thought. *I won't do that anymore.*

"Same," Peter answered.

"Well, that's good. We should be evenly matched then."

"Here's your club." Peter passed along the one that the clerk behind the counter had chosen for her. "And a ball. Which colour do you prefer?"

"I'll take the yellow one. Thanks." She reached for it, leaving him the orange one. "That one will be easy for you to find in the grass." She covered her smirk with her hand.

"Oh, you think I'm going to lose it in the grass? I'll take that as a challenge, so don't think I'm going to let you win," Peter teased.

"I wouldn't have it any other way. You won't have to let me win. I can win all by myself." Carmen lifted the club over her head as if she were lifting a barbell.

"Feeling pretty sure of yourself, eh?"

"Yup." Carmen headed to the first hole, which had a wooden Bugs Bunny eating a carrot at the side of the green. The peeling paint made it clear that it had sat through a few rainstorms.

"You can putt first, honey," Peter said.

Carmen smiled. That was the first time he had used an endearing term for her. "Okay, thanks." She bent to place the ball on the putting green, accentuating the lifting of one leg for balance. She knew he was watching her.

Carmen got the ball into the hole with only two strokes, which was par. "Okay, sexy man, your turn. Let's see you beat that."

"You're asking for it, lady." He hit the ball too hard, and it bounced off the wooden border and right back to him. "That doesn't count." He putted again.

"Oh, yes it does," Carmen said. "No sore losers."

This time, the ball hit at just the right angle to get into the hole with one stroke.

"What? What kind of sorcery was that?" Carmen said.

"No sorcery; just great skill," Peter bragged. He stood with his hands on his hips and his chest puffed out.

Carmen laughed so suddenly that she snorted. She covered her mouth with her hand and then turned around to hide.

"What was that, a snort? I thought you were a lady, not a little piggy."

Okay, he asked for it. I'm going to use a little of my own skills, Carmen thought. "Just move on to the next hole." She waved him over.

"Yes, ma'am."

She put the ball down and acted as if she had lost her balance and missed when she putted, but the ball swirled, swerved and headed right to the hole in the alligator's mouth.

"Now *that* looked like sorcery!" Peter exclaimed.

"That would mean that I am a sorceress."

"A sexy sorceress." He touched her as he walked to the tee. He took his shot, but the ball went out of control, circled around the hole twice and landed right in the corner of the boards. "That stank."

"That's for sure." Carmen tried not to laugh.

Peter tried again, and this time Carmen helped him out. After all, she didn't want him to look too bad. He hit the ball, and it went through the alligator's mouth, off the backboard and right into the hole.

"That was much better," she said.

They walked to the next hole, which had a pond with a fountain in the middle. *This should be fun*, Carmen thought.

"Go ahead, Carmen, give it your best shot."

Carmen took the golfer's pose, pointed her putter toward the hole, put it down on the green again, pointed at the hole again, and repeated this three times before turning to Peter and making a face.

"It's okay. I've got all day," he said. "That just means I spend more time with you."

"Aw." She cocked her head coyly. Finally, when she took her shot, the ball went into the water.

"That's okay, honey. The ball needed washing anyway."

Then, to Peter's amazement, the ball came up out of the other side of the pond and stopped on the green on the opposite side. "What the heck?" he sputtered.

Peter took his turn, and Carmen caused the ball to go up into the fountain and spin at the top of the water for several seconds until it popped off and landed right beside her ball.

"This is freaky," Peter said.

"You bet," Carmen said.

The rest of the game continued like this, and on the last hole, they both got holes-in-one. As they took their clubs back to the stand, they talked about the oddities that had occurred during their game.

"Did you have fun, Peter?"

"Yes, I always enjoy my time with you, but that was certainly fun. Did you have fun too?"

"For sure." *Especially watching you*, Carmen thought.

At the door of the little shack, a young man opened the door and shoved through before they could get out, so Carmen had the door hit him in the back of his heels.

Peter grabbed her hand and pulled her close to him.

Before he let her into the car, he stopped her, leaned her against the car door and kissed her. He ran his fingers through her hair and held her head so she looked directly into his eyes. "I love you, Carmen. I have for a very long time."

Carmen squeezed him tight. "I love you too, Peter."

"Will you stay with me tonight, Carmen?"

"I would love to." She smiled at him, and he opened the door for her.

"Do you want to stop at your place for anything?" Peter offered.

"That's a good idea."

When they got to Carmen's house, there was a message on the machine from her mother. "Do you see why I don't give her my cell phone number? Would you excuse me for a minute?" Carmen asked. She pressed the Play button.

"Carmen, I am utterly disappointed that you didn't see fit to show up at a family member's funeral. You are selfish and rude, and I am not at all surprised that you let me down again and embarrassed me in front of my family. Think on this for a while before you return my call, because if you call me now, I will let you have it full fury." The phone clicked, and she was gone.

"Well, that's my mother," Carmen said. "I'm sorry you had to hear that."

His mouth was agape. "Wow!"

"She's not going to ruin our day. Let's forget about her." Carmen gathered some things and headed back to the door. "I'm used to it. Her slap in the face doesn't sting much anymore." Carmen telepathically delivered a case of laryngitis to the hag on the other end of the phone line.

11

The message on Carmen's answering machine did not ruin their evening. Carmen had learned to let things her mother did roll off her back. She would have gone crazy long before if she hadn't. And she almost did, once.

She and Peter passionately kissed as soon as they walked in the front door of Peter's house. Peter was so attentive and affectionate. Carmen didn't have to think of how to act or what to do next; it all came naturally with Peter. He made her feel beautiful and sexy, so she had no insecurities with him.

He said all the right things. She replayed his saying 'I love you' by the car. It made her smile. *This is the best thing that has ever happened to me*, she thought. *I don't ever want it to stop. I want to have the life I have dreamed of having.*

Carmen woke once during the night, snuggled up tighter to Peter and fell asleep again.

They woke to the birds singing and lay in bed talking

until Carmen could hold her bladder no longer. She headed to the bathroom, and he headed downstairs.

"Tea time," Peter said when she joined him. "Where would you like to drink it?" He handed her a mug of tea just the way she liked it: strong with double milk and sugar.

"Is it warm enough outside yet?" Carmen asked.

"Let's find out." Peter held the door to the patio open. His backyard was lush with bushes and perennials. He had a little vegetable garden on the sunny side of the yard. Several different vegetables were growing there. He had a birdbath and a pond. Shelley ran to the pond to get a drink and then ran around looking for a spot to do her morning business.

"How would you like to go for a boat ride today?" Peter asked, readjusting himself in the chair. Shelley came back and sat beside him.

"Sure. What kind of boat do you want to ride, and where?" Carmen quizzed.

"How would you like to ride the paddle boats at the park?"

"Sounds like fun." Carmen took the last sip of her tea and put the mug down on the smoked-glass table.

Suddenly, a chipmunk came across the patio and sat up on its haunches watching them. "Stay, Shelley." Peter said to his beloved friend. "It's okay, buddy, you can come for breakfast." He got up and opened a large tin full of seeds and nuts. Shelley could hardly contain herself, but she held fast. Peter held the seeds in his hand, and the rodent nervously approached and snatched a peanut.

Stuffing it in his cheek, he grabbed another and another until his cheeks were full. Then the striped creature ran off with his tail erect around the corner of the house, disappearing under the bushes.

This man gets more and more perfect with every passing day, Carmen thought. *Pretty soon, I'll see a halo above his head. He is everything I want in a man.*

Peter proceeded to put a small plastic bag over his hand and head out to the back of the yard where Shelley had been. "Going poop hunting. Don't watch. It is humiliating for the master to clean up after his minion." He laughed.

Carmen smiled and covered her eyes dramatically with both hands but made a large gesture of widening her fingers, peeking between them and craning her neck to watch. "I had thought that if aliens ever looked at us, they would think that dogs were the superior species and we were the servants," Carmen told Peter when he came back to the patio.

"That's so true." Peter laughed. "We go to work, while they lay around. We feed them and pick up their crap. Oops, sorry."

"That's okay. I think I may have used that word once or twice myself." She laughed.

Shelley pranced around them, looking for some attention. "Yes, we are talking about you," Peter said.

Shelley barked.

Carmen looked around Peter's yard and granted the plants a little of her own unique fertilizer. Then she beckoned a pair of goldfinches to enhance Peter's Garden of Eden. She relished the look on Peter's face as he watched the birds flit around the birdbath and feeders.

"I hung my hummingbird feeder yesterday," Carmen said. "The ants were all over it already last night."

"I gave up on mine. The nectar was always a mess." Peter took a breath. "Well, shall we get ready for our boat ride? Do you want to bring Her Highness?"

Carmen answered, "Unquestionably. We couldn't leave her at home while we frolic. Well, we could, but I'd feel bad for her."

"Me too."

Shelley ran ahead of them as they returned to the house. They put their dishes in the sink and got ready for the boat ride.

"Do you want to go for a car ride, Shelley?" Peter said.

The dog's tail wagged hard, and she ran in small circles and then headed to the front door.

"Nah, she doesn't want to go." Carmen chuckled.

When they arrived at the park, people were already out on the boats.

"Wow, we weren't the only ones with this idea today," Peter remarked as they reached the pond. He had to hold Shelley's leash tightly because she strained against it excitedly. "Shelley, heel!" Peter demanded. She settled down immediately, standing still beside his right leg.

"You have trained her very well," Carmen affirmed. "She listens remarkably well to you."

"We worked hard at your training, didn't we, Shelley?" He patted her head.

Peter paid for a boat, and the kid at the dock got one

ready for them. Peter held Carmen's hand and helped her get in. She sat in the far seat and took Shelley when Peter handed her the leash and lifted the little pup into the boat. Carmen tried to settle the boat while Peter got in, but it rocked until he sat down. The kid on the dock pushed the boat gently out into the pond.

Shelley sat still, sniffing the air, while Peter pedalled first to turn the boat in the right direction, and then he and Carmen both pedalled to go straight. The warm breeze blew through their hair and the dog's fur as they propelled the boat as fast as they could. They struggled to keep up the pace and lost momentum when they started laughing. As they laughed, the dog barked.

So, when they tired, they coasted for a while, Carmen dipping her fingers in the water. Carp came up to investigate and startled her since she hadn't known they were there. She laughed, and when Peter laughed too, she flicked the water from her fingertips into his face.

"Eww!" he protested. "That's yucky pond water."

"Yucky?" Carmen teased.

"Yeah, yucky. Foul, gross, filthy, repulsive, disgusting, revolting, sickening—"

"Okay, I get the idea. I was just teasing you because you used a childlike word."

"Well, I try not to use foul language in front of you. I am trying to be a gentleman, you know."

"And you are doing a great job," Carmen said, and she flicked more water at him.

"Hey! We are not amused," he said in a mock British accent.

Carmen pulled a face. "Okay, that's taking the gentleman thing a little far."

Shelley was trying to get a closer look—or sniff, as it were—at the carp and their gaping mouths at the surface of the water. Peter held her tight to keep her from falling into the pond. "Nothing worse than a wet dog."

"That's for sure. That would be freaking disgusting." Carmen chuckled.

"Smelly, for sure. Then you would need a bath, wouldn't you, princess? And we all know you hate that, don't we?"

Shelley whimpered at the word *bath*.

"It's okay. Just don't fall in the yucky water." Peter looked to Carmen for her response. He smirked when she made a face. "Well, shall we start pedalling again?"

They floated around the pond for a while until Carmen noticed that Peter's nose was getting red. "Here, let me put some sunblock on you." Carmen got out her bottle of SPF30 and squeezed a tiny dab onto her hand. With a fingertip, she spread the lotion onto his nose.

Peter made an exaggerated cross-eyed expression that made her laugh. She loved how playful he was.

"Can I put some of that on you?" Peter took the bottle from her and poured a bit onto his palm. "Here, let's start with your cheeks, and then we'll do your neck, and your shoulders, and here and here." He traced a finger from the hollow of her neck down the crease of her cleavage and up over the curve of one of her breasts. He slowed his fingers and, looking into her eyes, cupped her breast tenderly.

Carmen felt the heat intensify. She leaned forward to

kiss his waiting lips. He welcomed her kiss and returned the offering.

"Get a room!" a boy on the shore yelled, startling them out of the moment.

"Watch out for the shore!" another boy shouted.

Embarrassed, Peter and Carmen sat back and resumed pedalling, Peter going first to turn away from the rock wall at the shore. "Well, should we return to the dock?" he asked.

"I think that was long enough," Carmen responded. "I'm feeling a little windblown."

"I bet Shelley needs to pee."

"She's not the only one," Carmen said.

"We'll find a nice patch of grass for both of you," Peter teased.

"I thought you were trying to be a gentleman. That was certainly a failed attempt." Carmen stuck her tongue out at him. "But if we don't hurry, I might not make it past the grass."

As soon as they reached the shore, Shelley jumped off the boat and headed for the grass. "I knew it." Peter nodded.

Carmen and Peter docked the boat and gave the rope to the attendant. They followed Shelley up to the little snack shop.

"Would you like something to eat?" Peter asked. "It's not the healthiest stuff, but it tastes good."

They decided on hotdogs and even shared with Shelley, who gobbled her portion down without chewing. "You pig, Shelley. If you choke on a wiener, I'm not doing the Heimlich on you."

"Me neither," Carmen said. "And no mouth to mouth. You're on your own. I draw the line at bad breath, big teeth and wet noses."

Peter laughed. "I draw the line at long snouts."

"Aww, poor thing. We're making fun of her and she doesn't even know it." Carmen crumpled her hotdog wrapper. Shelley watched her throw it in the garbage can.

She then turned to Peter as he crumpled his wrapper. A piece of onion fell out, and Shelley dove at it, catching it almost before it hit the ground.

"I guess she believes in the five-second rule," Carmen reported.

"She doesn't discriminate. She follows the five-hour rule. Oops, there we go, making fun of you again, eh, girl?" Peter stroked Shelley under her chin.

Carmen then heard the snack shop employee grumble to a disheveled, skinny man looking for handouts, "Get lost. There's nothing for free here. And stay out of the garbage cans, too."

The man left and sat on a bench not far away. Carmen went over to the employee. "One order of hotdog, fries and milk, please."

"Sure," the employee said, taking her money.

"You know, we don't choose our destinies. You could have been born into that man's life. Plus, someone else might look down at you."

"Don't hound me, lady. He scares customers away." The man handed the tray of food to Carmen.

"He didn't scare *me* away."

Carmen brought the tray to the man on the bench.

The man hesitated, but then smiled, took the tray and thanked her.

"That was a very nice thing to do," Peter said when she returned. "I'm proud of you."

Shelley had followed Carmen to the snack shop, to the man on the bench and back to Peter again, her tail wagging all the time.

Peter took Carmen's hand, kissed it and led her back to the car. "Is there anywhere else you'd like to go?"

"Would a walk in the woods be okay?"

"Of course, that would be nice," Peter said.

They spent the next couple of hours strolling through the woods. Shelley, led by her nose, scampering ahead of them, then behind them, all the time running and bouncing over fallen trees. They had a wonderful afternoon, enjoying the gentle breeze blowing the leaves on the trees, birds singing and water rippling down the little creek. They sat for a while on a rock and watched Shelley chase the butterflies that Carmen conjured up.

Later they spent the evening sitting by the fire pit in Peter's backyard, where she summoned a hooting owl to keep them company.

"I've never had an owl in my yard before," Peter said.

"Do you like it?" Carmen suddenly caught herself.

Peter looked at her. "As if you had something to do with it." He chuckled.

What the heck? She decided to play along. "Of course. Birds follow me everywhere, especially the raptors. It's the smell of the hospital that I carry on me." She laughed.

"You smell like lavender most of the time," Peter informed her.

"That's my body wash. Lavender is my favourite." She stroked her arms.

"It's supposed to be relaxing, isn't it?"

Carmen wondered how he knew that. "Yes. So if you fall asleep while you're with me, I won't take offence." She chuckled.

"The thought of sleeping with you is very inviting," he confessed with a sparkle in his eye.

"As is the thought of sleeping with *you*. Shall we go in before we're so tired that all we do is sleep?"

"Oh, yeah." Peter leaped from his seat.

All, in all it was a perfect day.

12

Carmen and Lara had arranged to get together to shop for baby things the next day, so Carmen picked her friend up and drove to the mall.

Another car cut them off in the parking lot, so Carmen fashioned a little trick to make the driver's side window go up and down until the cretin parked and turned his car off.

At the doorway of the mall, some children were pointing at and taunting a man with the bumpy skin of neurofibromatosis. A young woman stopped the children and said that they were cruel and should be more considerate of others' feelings because anything could be in store for them as well.

Carmen used her fabulous gift to help the man with his suffering and hoped that she was strong enough to make all the bumps disappear. Then, she gave a temporary bout of acne to each of the teasing youngsters and finally a gift of glowing skin to the woman who stuck up for the man.

Lara commented on the malicious events but didn't

notice any of the changes Carmen brought about. Her secret was still safe, and they continued into the mall.

They stepped into a baby boutique, but, awestruck by the prices, moved on to another store. The next store had a sale on, and some things weren't too expensive, so they picked up a few items the baby would need right off. However, in the department store, they found the best prices and some cute soft sleepers in pastel colours, bibs for all seven days of the week and a stroller at half price. They also bought flannelette receiving blankets, socks and cotton onesies.

Carmen dreamed of the day when she would be shopping for her own baby. Peter's baby.

They had a pleasant morning, and when they stopped for a coffee, Peter called. "Hi, Honey," Carmen said. "Yes, we are having a fun time. We found some good deals and adorable things. I can't talk right now, okay? I don't want to be rude to Lara. Okay, bye."

"You seem so happy when you hear from him. Do you think he might be the one?" Lara asked.

"He sure is looking that way. I can only hope so." Carmen put her phone back in her purse.

"Well, you deserve it."

"That is kind of you to say." Carmen took the last sip of her coffee.

"Carmen, you are a super woman, and any man would be blessed to have you."

"Thanks. That means a lot to me. I've travelled a long road trying to find someone, yet he was under my nose for years."

"Are you recharged? Shall we shop more?"

"Sure. Raring to go." Carmen stood up and gathered some of the bags.

They tried two more stores but found nothing else, so they returned to the car.

"Would you like to get a drink at the drive-through?" Carmen asked. "I know I'm thirsty."

"Only if you let me treat since you drove."

"Well, I think you spent enough money today, don't you?" Carmen laughed.

"I spent a bundle, that's for sure."

"Are you scared at all?" Carmen said suddenly. "I mean of the delivery and then raising this little creature."

"Yes, very much, but people do it every day, so it can't be that bad. I just hope all is well and that instinct will take over." Lara rubbed her belly.

Carmen willed that all would be well for her, granting her a healthy baby, an easy delivery and the wisdom to raise her child.

After spending a pleasant day with Lara, Carmen returned home. The house was quiet and peaceful, and for a short time she sat alone with her thoughts.

She relived her dad's recent appearance, and while she felt happy to have him back in her life, she still viewed the sudden homecoming with a degree of suspicion. He had debased her trust, his obligation to her, despite whatever he or her mother said. She knew it would take time for her to sort everything out. Deciding on filling Jill in, she went to the phone and called her sister.

"I only have a minute," Jill said, sounding hurried. "We're heading out to Bradley's soccer practice."

"Dad contacted me," Carmen said quickly, not wanting to lose Jill to the soccer practice. She had to talk to Jill. She had to confess what nasty thing she had done years before, and certainly, Jill was the only one that she could tell.

"No kidding!" Jill exclaimed. "When? Where has he been all these years? Why come back into your life now? And what about me?"

"Okay, okay." Carmen didn't feel like she had time to answer all the questions and make her confession as well. "I didn't tell you that he was here. I'll explain more later. I just have to get something off my chest."

"What is it?"

"I put a curse on Dad a long time ago."

"What did you do to him?" Jill asked, sounding less pressed for time now.

"Well, when he left, we heard all the mean things Mom could possibly have told us, and of course we believed her. I was angry with him, Jill. I thought only the worst of him. We were teenagers, and I lashed out at him the only way that I knew how. He wasn't there to defend himself or to justify his actions."

"Really! What did you do to him?" Jill said.

"I gave him the curse ... that no one would ever love him." She broke down in tears. She covered her face with her hand and sobbed. "I'm a monster. Mom was right." She cried. "Then he comes to my door, a dear, sweet man telling me how Mom chased him away. He has been alone and unloved all these years, Jill, and I did that to him. I had a lovely evening with him and totally disregarded what I had done to him until today. It hit me like a brick wall. How could I have even done what I did?"

"I don't know what to say, Carmen. I have to go to Bradley's practice now. We can talk later. Okay? I love you. Don't be too hard on yourself. You were young and misinformed." She hung up the phone.

Carmen just sat there, wiping her tears, running her hands up and down her arms, and rocking in the chair, trying to console herself. *I want Peter*, she thought, *but I can't even tell him.*

How ironic it is that I should curse him and be the unloved one myself for all this time? Even when I think I have found love, I have to fight for it. The power that made it possible for me to curse my father to be alone also curses me.

The image of her grandmother came to her mind, and this just made her feel worse. *Grandma, you aren't here for me either. What should I do?*

What about Dad? Maybe I should call him and talk to him. But how can I tell him what I did? How can I make up for the love I stole from him? Carmen thought for a moment. She paced the floor several times.

She picked up the phone again. "I need to tell you something," she began when the call was answered. "I did something awful, something I should have never done. I am generally a good person, and usually I do things to help others or change others."

She switched the phone to her other ear. "But the fault is yours. You made me do it."

There was only silence at the other end.

"So, I never want to see you or hear from you again.

You have treated me badly, and I will no longer take that from you. You have lied to me and caused me too much pain.

"Mother, do you hear me?"

There was no answer.

"Dad came to me. You lied and sent him out of Jill's life and mine. We missed so much. You are the one who earned loneliness. I curse you with that. The curse I put on Dad is now on you. No one will ever love you. Not that you need a curse for that. You do that just fine on your own."

Carmen hung up the phone, completely surprised with herself. She let out a long sigh. "I need a glass of wine. A huge one."

Carmen was almost breathless. Adrenaline surged through her veins. She tried to calm herself. Sitting down, she sipped her wine and closed her eyes. Then the tears came. She hated that she cried whenever she calmed down from being upset. She wiped her tears briskly. *Was I too harsh?* she asked herself.

She turned on the TV to distract herself. She came across an old movie that she had seen years ago. It was a wholesome movie about a family in the times of the pioneers that worked together, laughed together and cried together.

Carmen loved movies like this one. She wished she had been part of a big happy family. *Well, maybe I can make my own.*

A commercial came on, so Carmen got up to make a cup of tea. Through the window, she saw Allan. Feeling as if she had been using her gift wrongly, she granted Allan healing, and she was content with her decision.

I will take the curse off my mother, too. No one deserves to be unloved. I made a mistake with that curse once already. I will not do it again. And with that, she removed the curse from her mother as well. *It's nine o'clock. She'll be in bed reading.*

Peter should be home from work by now. I think I'll call him. There was no answer on his home phone, so she called his cell. She heard it ringing outside. He had been just about to knock on her door.

"Hello, beautiful!" he said when she opened the door. "Were you expecting me?"

"No, I just heard your phone ringing," Carmen explained.

"Wow, you have good ears."

"Come in," she said, stepping aside. She threw her arms around him and kissed him. "I'm glad you're here. Come in the kitchen. I just poured some wine."

"Good. I didn't want to be pushy, but I missed you today. Even when I can't see you, it's nice to know at least that you're in the same building as I am, so I missed you even more today. Could I have tea instead? Did you do anything interesting on your day off?"

"Well, I went shopping with Lara." Carmen filled the kettle.

"Oh yeah. Sorry; I forgot. How was that?"

"Good. We shopped for baby stuff." Carmen put a tea bag into a mug and turned to face him.

"Oh, right, she's having a baby. Did you do anything else?"

"I had a big row with my mother." Carmen poured the boiling water into the mug. "I confronted her about her lying about my dad."

"Did she admit to it?" Peter asked.

"She barely said a word. Even when I told her I never wanted to see her again."

"Ouch! Are you sure that's what you want?"

"They say to stay away from people who are toxic to you." Carmen handed Peter his tea.

"Well, you know her better than I do. I just wouldn't want you to regret it later."

"Let's go sit down. Do you want to watch some TV? I have it on already."

"What are you watching?" Peter asked as he sat in the corner of the couch.

"I'm watching an old corny movie." Carmen curled up beside him.

"Oh, I love this commercial," Peter chimed. "That dog is so funny."

Carmen laughed. "I haven't seen that one before. It's good." Another commercial came on the screen.

"But this one stinks. Who would ever believe that?" Peter retorted.

"Bogus advertising drives me nuts. The products don't do what they say they will, and some claims are just blatant lies that only a fool would believe."

"I know. There are so many scams out there. Still, somebody is getting rich from them."

"Would you like more tea?" Carmen offered.

"No, thanks. I'm good." He smiled at her. "Isn't there

a company that regulates commercials? I mean, one that checks for the truth."

"Hey, if we can't keep our politicians honest, who would bother trying to keep the truth in advertising?" Carmen said. "Yeah, there is Advertising Standards Canada, but the commercials and products are always one step ahead."

"I've seen this movie before, a long time ago," Peter said. "It *is* a corny one." He chuckled.

"Do you want me to look for something else?"

"No, it's okay. I like the old ones." He nestled into the couch cushions and pulling Carmen closer.

"I love you, Peter."

"I love you too, Carmen." He turned and kissed her on her forehead.

Norma propped herself up in bed, a glass of whiskey and the bottle of prescription sleeping pills that she had just refilled yesterday at the pharmacy on the nightstand. She picked up a pad of paper and scribbled:

> You're right, Carmen. Nobody loves me. Your dad walked out on me, and you and Jill hate me for it. I have been an awful mother to you.
>
> I was never truly jealous of the power you have, though, because I have it too. But I had to promise your father that I

would give it up when I married him. He would have no part of any of that.

But he did not seem to mind that you used yours. I resented him for that. Then, after he walked out, I continued to keep from using the powers, hoping that he would someday come back.

But why would he? I am just a crusty and miserable woman.

She took a sip of whiskey and then emptied the entire bottle of little blue pills into her hand. She thumbed through them. *This should be enough to do the job right. I wouldn't want to fail and just become a vegetable. Maybe I should mix some pain pills in, too.* She reached into the nightstand for the analgesics, opened the bottle and poured them into her hand too.

She watched the digital clock turn to 9:00, and suddenly she felt different. She shook her head, looked at the handful of pills and put them back into the bottle. She didn't want to do this. *She took the curse off me again. I don't feel it anymore.*

She crumpled up the note she had written and threw it into the wastepaper basket. *I need to make amends with my girls. Now that their dad is back, maybe I can make a fresh start.*

She picked up her book and opened it to where she had left off the night before.

In the meantime, Jill heard from their father as well. She had felt a little left out since she had heard that their father had contacted Carmen but not her.

"I hope you don't mind that Carmen gave your phone number to me," he said. "I would like to come and see you in person. I want to start over. Carmen says you have children, my grandchildren. May we start over, Jill?"

Jill was unsure, but she trusted Carmen. The fact that she had allowed their father into *her* life helped Jill to make up her mind. "Yes, I think we could do that …" She hesitated, but then finally said, "Dad."

Carmen and Peter were spending the next evening watching Shelley and the cat play. Shelley chased Oscar around the family room. Then the cat sat on the chair and swatted at the dog when she lay on the floor just out of reach. Peter and Carmen got a good laugh.

The cat jumped on Carmen's lap and meowed. "Oh, I know," Carmen said. "And men are just like dogs." The cat rubbed against Carmen. "Now *you* are being just like a man, rubbing against me like that." She looked at Peter, who pulled a face and made her laugh again.

Shelley, not to be left out, jumped onto Peter's lap. "Shelley, you are a bit too boney and heavy to be jumping on my lap." He nudged her off.

"Aww, poor thing. She's feeling neglected, aren't

you, baby? Here, sit between us." She patted the cushion between herself and Peter as she slid over.

Peter scowled and repositioned himself as the wiggling dog jumped back up and shimmed between them. "Sorry, Shelley. You just don't smell as good as Carmen does."

Carmen chuckled, stroking the long-haired dog. In the meantime, Oscar had jumped down and run to the kitchen, probably disliking the restlessness on the couch.

"My dad contacted Jill," Carmen declared out of nowhere. "She wasn't sure at first what to do, but she has agreed to meet with him. So I suggested we meet him together."

"That's a good idea," Peter said. "Wow, after all these years."

"I know." Carmen sighed. "It's exciting."

"I must commend you, Carmen. A lot of people would tell him to go to hell. I'm not sure what I would do."

"I'm giving him the benefit of the doubt because of my mother's character." Carmen stretched her legs. "I should go home. I have to work tomorrow." She stood up, grabbed her purse and headed for the door.

"Why the fast exit?" Peter asked as he followed her.

"I just got a funny feeling about my mother." Carmen kissed him quickly.

She quickly went to her car and got in. It wouldn't start at the first turn of the key, so she forced it to start using her mind.

She realized that she had done a lot of speeding lately.

As Carmen reached her front steps, her cell phone rang.

"Is this Carmen Hamilton?" the voice on the other end asked.

"Yes. Something's wrong with my mother, isn't it?" Carmen stated.

"I'm calling from the hospital. Your mother has been in an accident. She was hit by a car and is in the Intensive Care Unit. How did you know?"

Carmen gasped. "I'll be right there." She spun on her heels and headed back to her car. When she got to the hospital, she remembered why she walked to work. The parking garage was damp and creepy, and it was difficult to find a parking space.

Carmen ran through the hospital until she reached the ICU. There she found her mother bandaged, tubed, wired and in a leg cast.

"Mom!" she cried.

"What are you doing here? I thought you never wanted to see me again."

"Well, certainly not like this," Carmen responded. "What happened?"

"I got hit by a car."

"Just you, or were you in your car?"

"Just me."

"How?"

"Enough questions."

"Mother!"

"I stepped off the curb and got hit, okay?" Norma said, annoyed.

"Mother, do you always have to be so cantankerous? I'm just trying to wrap my head around this."

"I ran into your father downtown today. It surprised me. I tried to avoid him, and I was too distracted to realize what I was doing and stepped off the curb in front of a car." Norma grimaced as she shifted herself in bed.

"Did you talk to Dad?" Carmen asked.

"Of course not." She suspended her next words, as the nurse came in the room.

"How are you doing, Mrs. Hamilton?" the nurse asked pleasantly.

"Ms."

"Pardon?" the nurse questioned politely.

"It's Ms., and I only kept the last name for my daughter's sake," Norma snapped.

The nurse turned and Carmen noticed her roll her eyes.

"Oh, hi, Carmen," she said uncomfortably. "Is this your mother?"

"Hi, Sue. Unfortunately, yes," Carmen half-heartedly joked.

"How are you keeping?" Sue asked.

"Fine, thanks. You?"

"Good." The nurse left the room.

"Mom, are you all right? You look lost in thought."

"I'm all right," Norma said. "I want things to be different. I want to be a better person. I want a better relationship with you and Jill, and perhaps even with your father."

"Now, Mom, most of that sounds great, but do you really think there is even the slightest chance with Dad? I mean, you sent him running and then completely lied about him. He's no fool."

"Carmen, the other night I wrote a letter to you confessing things that you don't know about. I was unfair to you about your gift. I wasn't jealous that you had the gift; I was jealous that you could use yours but I couldn't use mine." She paused to watch for Carmen's reaction.

Carmen shook her head. "What? What gift are you talking about?"

Norma stopped playing with her hospital armband and looked straight at Carmen. "I have the same power as you, Carmen. But your father wanted nothing to do with it and forbade me to use it."

"You have the same ability? Why didn't you ever tell me? So it's genetic? Who else has this skill?"

"My father, your grandpa, had it. He used it differently than you do, though. Only for himself, when no one was looking. He used it to lessen his workload, but he kept it under wraps. Grandpa didn't want to be thought of as strange."

"Well, his and your keeping it hush-hush made me feel like I was strange. Why didn't *he* ever tell me? He was selfish to keep it to himself. What about Grandma? I believed we were close, but she kept it all a secret from me too. Now I feel like I don't know any of you. I feel betrayed!" Carmen stood and paced. "I can't believe this. All these years of feeling like a freak. Someone could have helped me!"

"Carmen, I don't want you to feel that way. You keep it a secret, too, don't you?"

Carmen looked out the window, down at the people walking up the path. "Well, if I saw that my child had it,

I would celebrate it with her, explain it to her and make sure that she understood herself." Carmen turned from the window. Mascara streaked her face as she cried. "I have to go. I have a lot to think about." She wiped her face on her sleeve. *I haven't been this angry in a long time, and again it is my mother's fault.* She walked out the door without saying goodbye.

Carmen walked down the hallway, oblivious to her surroundings.

"Bye, Carmen," Sue said, but her words fell on deaf ears.

The sun was just above the horizon. Orange and pink streaks etched the sky and silhouetted the willow trees by the pond. Carmen and Peter watched the swans and the people enjoying the gentle breeze on their faces. Shelley's fur blew, and she sat facing the breeze to keep the fur out of her eyes, until Carmen spoke. She turned toward Carmen's voice.

"Peter, I want to tell you something."

Peter looked up at Carmen, who had been quiet for a while. "What is it, honey? You sound so serious. I hope there isn't anything wrong. I'm sorry, you wanted to say something. Go ahead."

"I said that I want to tell you something. Something … about me." She paused. "Do you remember that I told you that I was different?"

"Yes, and I argued with you," Peter responded.

"I didn't want to talk about it then, but I do now."

"What's to talk about? I already told you that you're exceptional," Peter reminded her.

"I have the ability to manipulate events," Carmen said.

"What?" Peter looked stunned and shifted on the bench. Shelley had settled down by his feet and stirred when he moved.

Carmen tucked her wind-blown hair behind her ears, attempting to keep her eyes visible to Peter. "Watch." She caused a man's hat to blow off.

"Watch what?" Peter asked.

"I made that man's hat blow off."

"What are you talking about? The wind blew his hat off. You sound a little silly." Peter leaned back and looked at her strangely.

So, trying to prove her point, she made the litter on the ground swirl around the garbage can and then fall into it.

Peter looked at her, tilting his head.

"Remember the speeder whose car broke down? I made it stall," Carmen said. "And do you recall the litterer on the beach? I made the candy wrapper fly up into the kid's face. The owl in your yard. Do you recollect when we were talking about justice and karma, when you quoted Beatrix Potter?"

"I remember, but I don't follow. You're making it sound like you have supernatural powers. That's just insane."

"I give people back what they deserve," Carmen clarified.

"And who gave you that authority?" Peter said, pulling away from her.

"I don't know. It just seemed to be my calling. You know that people love to watch the bad guy in the movies get it."

"But that's the movies, Carmen. This is real life."

A boy was struggling to ride his bicycle up the hill. Carmen pointed to him. "See that boy? Watch him." She concentrated, and suddenly the boy easily pedalled his bike up the hill. "I just want to be honest and upfront with you. I know how it feels when people aren't honest."

"How did you get this … this power, or whatever you call it? How long have you had it? Have you manipulated me in any way?" Peter stammered. Suddenly, as if a light bulb had turned on, he said, "So *you* did that to Allan Roberts! How do I know you won't break my ankle?"

"Slow down, Peter. I was born this way. I learned as a child how to use it. I have only gifted you with owls, fireflies, flowers and such. But I must confess, I caused Allan to fall and break his ankle. I was just so angry when I saw him out on bail." Carmen touched Peter's hand and looked down.

He pulled his hand back and looked concerned. "What if you get mad at me? Are you going to break my leg too?" He stood up and turned away. "I don't get this. No wonder your father ran and your mother was ashamed of you. You are a freak."

Tears streamed down Carmen's face. She had heard that word before, but it never hurt any less. If anything, the repetition pained her more deeply. "My mother has this power too. Just give it time to sink in. I usually use my gift for good, like what I did for the boy on the bicycle. And here, watch." Carmen beckoned the swans to come to her. They looked up, stood up and walked toward her.

Peter backed away. "These are swans, Carmen, not chickadees. They can be vicious."

"They are fine."

He looked at Shelley and then at Carmen. "Do you control my dog too?" Peter sounded defensive and distrustful. "You are manipulative. You force people to like you."

"I do not. Most people don't like me once they find out, just like you. And as for Shelley, she connects with me. I don't control her. Isn't that right, Shelley?"

The dog sat up and nudged Carmen's hand.

"This is too weird for me. I have got to go. You are a freakin' witch! Come on, Shelley." Peter picked up the little dog as if defending her and claiming her as his. He began walking to his car.

"But, Peter, you drove me here!" Carmen felt sick to her stomach as she walked after him.

"No way. Call a cab. Or fly on your broomstick. You're not getting in my car with me. I've seen what you do to cars."

"Peter, please don't freak out. I'm still me. I'm no different than the girl you loved fifteen minutes ago."

But he said nothing.

After two days, Carmen still hadn't heard from Peter. She couldn't concentrate on her work, so she left early. As soon as she got home, she called Jill and told her what had happened.

"Give him time," Jill suggested. "Give him his space and some time to think."

"I've lost him." Carmen cried. "He called me a witch, and manipulative. He said that was why Dad left and why Mom is ashamed of me. He left me there and told me to call a cab."

"Then it wasn't meant to be," Jill answered softly.

"Maybe I should take it all back. Tell him that I was just fooling around."

"Then he'll think you're nuts. Just leave it be."

"This has always been a curse on me. I am just going to quit using my ability, that's all. I'll tell him that I'll stop using it, just for him." Carmen stood up, looked out the window and relaxed her shoulders. "That's all I have to do."

"Carmen, what about all the good you do? And you need someone who can accept *all* of you."

"I'll never find someone who will accept this. This is my karma, for the curse on Dad, for what I did to Allan. I have been doing some petty and nasty things. That will all stop. I have to go." Carmen was about to hang up the phone, but then she waited to hear the rest of what Jill was saying.

"Carmen, don't go calling Peter begging for him

back," Jill said quickly. "That will just turn him off more. Give him more time. Please, trust me with this one. You aren't thinking clearly. Promise me."

"Okay, Jill. Thanks." Carmen hung up the phone and turned away from it before she was tempted to pick it up and call another number.

Peter was shocked by Carmen's revelation. It also scared him partially because he believed she could do what she said she could do. *Have I fallen in love with a witch?* he wondered. The idea made his blood turn cold. He was also afraid of what she could do to him. *She could destroy me.*

Not wanting to see her at work, he called in sick and paced around his house for a day. Finally, feeling totally depressed, hurt, angry, anxious, confused and betrayed, he called his mom for advice. She had always been a steadying hand.

His drive to her house was all a blur. He was barely able to focus on the road.

Rachel met him on the driveway. "I was so worried. You sounded so down, so I just waited for you to get here." She hugged him, linked her arm in his and led him silently into the house.

"Mom, I don't know what to do. I thought things were going so well," Peter confided. He plopped his weary body down on the couch.

"Things *were* going well, darling. I'm sure everything is all right." She sat beside him.

"I don't know. Carmen has this weird thing about her, a secret. She told me all about it. She isn't who I thought she was." Peter squeezed a cushion to his belly.

"Of course she is. I think she is a lovely girl. Besides, we all have something weird about us." Rachel smiled, but her smile faded as she looked at his sad face. "We all make mistakes."

"It isn't just a weird thing. It's almost supernatural." Peter looked away from his mother's direct gaze. "You don't even know what it is, and you're taking her side."

"It can't be that bad, can it? Why don't you tell me?" She folded her hands on her lap.

"I can't." Peter thrust out his arms, sending the pillow bouncing on the floor. He stood up, walked around the couch and sat down when his mother spoke again.

"Because you want to keep her secret in case there is still a future with her. You hope there is still a future with her." Rachel kissed him on the cheek.

"Of course I hope there is a future with her." He paused. "I love her. I've been thinking about how we would make a life together." Peter picked up the pillow and put it back in the corner of the couch. "I want a family, like we had with Dad. I want to give you grandchildren. I want big family gatherings at the holidays. I want to see the world with her. Share the ups and downs with her …" Then, softly and gently, he added, "Love her." Tears welled in his eyes, and Rachel put her arm around him.

"I thought you both suited each other well," Rachel said, rubbing his back. "I don't know everything between you, and I can't decide your future for you. But when you love someone, forgiveness is the key. Will talking to her help? Knowing you, you've probably given her the cold shoulder. Has she been trying to contact you?"

"Yes, and you're right about the cold shoulder." He succumbed to her back stroking. He loved the tenderness his mother showed him. He had always felt safe with her. She was smart and wise, and she and his dad had been so much in love. She knew how to make a marriage work. He had shared her pain when his father died, and they had become closer because of it.

Peter had never loved someone as much as he loved Carmen, and it had taken him so long to finally begin a relationship with her. He couldn't bear seeing her at the hospital or on the street. He felt like he would have to move away. He shook his head. He didn't want to do any of that. His life was here, in this town, near his mother, working at the hospital and loving the woman of his dreams.

He stood. "Thanks, Mom."

"I hope I helped you, son."

"You did."

"Now go home and get some sleep. You have bags under your eyes." Rachel stood up and grabbed his hands to pull him up off the couch.

Peter thought about Carmen the whole way home. He missed her. He loved her. But what if she turned against him and used her abilities on him?

Since she had been honest with him, he would have to be honest with her. But his vice merited punishment. It would be completely acceptable for her to chastise him. He contemplated how she would react to *his* secret.

13

Carmen was having a hard time getting through her day at work. The usual politics were extremely noticeable while she felt down.

Tina was especially happy to see Carmen feeling blue. "Trouble in paradise?" she said sarcastically. "Gee, I didn't see that one coming!"

"Shut up, Tina," Carmen finally said, after years of wanting to. With a swift gesture of Carmen's hand, the seat of Tina's overstretched pants split down the middle.

Tina heard the tear, and with wide eyes, she put her hands behind her and trotted down the hallway to find another pair of scrubs as fast as she could carry her oversized rump.

"What you put out into the world comes back to you," Carmen said.

Luckily, no patients had been in the hallway to overhear their unprofessional behaviour. But Carmen could not take anymore.

Then, to top it off, she heard one of the nurses praising

herself for her work. *It just doesn't end. When you do good things, you aren't supposed to pat yourself on the back.*

"Diana, this place is driving me nuts," Carmen said. "Is it just me, or is it getting bad here?"

"Tina has become out of control," Diana responded. "She's dragging morale down and just gets after you because you had her suspended. We can never change her character. We just have to manage how we react to her, which is almost impossible, but it's necessary for our own sanity."

After work, feeling so forlorn, Carmen stepped into one of the churches in the neighbourhood.

The lights were dim, but the sun shone through the stained glass windows. The colours were lovely. The deep red carpet and padded pews were a little garish but inviting. Artificial flowers in large urns had been placed around the church.

Carmen saw a man at the front of the chapel. As she approached, she heard him practicing his sermon. He looked up at her and stopped, putting his papers on the pulpit.

"Reverend, I just have to talk to someone. Do you have a minute?" Carmen asked.

"Sure," the baby-faced blond minister said.. "You aren't a parishioner here, though, are you? Not that it matters. I just know I haven't seen you here before. Have a seat." He pointed to the first pew, and they sat.

"No, I don't go to church. I never have, so I have a hard time fitting into a congregation."

"Yes, it takes time to feel at ease with new people, but

you are welcome anytime. Anyway, you wanted to talk about something?"

"Well, I wanted to talk to you about punishment."

"Oh?" he responded.

She continued, "I have been let down lately, lost a love, and been betrayed by my mother, and even my late grandparents. I feel as though I'm being punished. Have I brought this upon myself?" Carmen looked into his kind eyes, hoping for a little reassurance.

"God lays out challenges for us but does not punish us per se. There are consequences for the things we do. Some events are caused by others, and there is nothing we can do about them. God allows things to happen because he gives all of us free will. What is it that you think you've done to justify this punishment?" He laid his arm across the back of the pew.

"Is this conversation confidential?" Carmen probed as she looked around for other people.

"Yes, certainly, as long as it isn't about something illegal or hurting a minor. Do you have children?"

"No, I don't. I hope to someday. But I've lost the person I was hoping to have those children with. I told him something about myself, and he has avoided me since."

"May I ask what you told him?" the minister inquired.

"I told him about a special skill I have." She squeezed her purse in her lap.

The minister's eyes widened, and a bewildered look crossed his face.

"I have the ability to engineer occurrences, and I use

them to reward or punish people." She rubbed her hands together, feeling awkward.

"I don't understand ... By the way, what is your name?"

"Carmen."

"I am Simon. Pleased to meet you." He stretched out his hand, and she shook it. They both smiled.

"Okay, I'll show you what I was talking about." She manipulated the minister's papers to rise from the pulpit, swirl in the air and coast to his hands.

His mouth fell open as he looked from his papers to her. "I have never seen anything like that. I didn't know anyone had that power, that it was even possible."

"I do, and I just found out that my mother and grandfather had it too."

"Would you call it telekinesis?" he asked.

"I guess that's the closest name for it."

"So what kind of rewards and punishments do you carry out?" He sounded curious like a child.

"I have gifted butterflies, fragrances, peace." She paused to think. "Self-esteem, money, patience and healing."

"What? You can heal people?"

"To some degree. I don't proclaim to be a healer." Carmen readjusted herself on the pew. "I can ease people's suffering, but I don't know how long the effect lasts. I cured my grandmother of cancer, but I haven't been able to cure anyone else."

"That is fascinating," Simon said.

"I was never able to cure my mother's unpleasant personality." She chuckled, but then regretted having said that. "In the line of punishments, I have caused cars to break down, given people rashes and headaches, and even caused a burglar to fall and break his ankle."

The minister's eyes widened. He scratched his head.

Carmen wondered if that was nervousness. "So, anyway, I told my boyfriend about these skills, and he panicked. I haven't heard from him in three days."

"It sure could be overwhelming for a man to realize his girlfriend has this much power. Men like to be the strong ones, the protectors. Hopefully, he is doing some research on telekinesis as we speak. I know I will be. Have you tried calling him?"

"No, my sister suggested I give him some time."

"Well, three days seems adequate to me. Call him and see what happens." He stood up. "I need to go home for supper. My wife is expecting me at five o'clock. I hope I was of some help to you, Carmen. You have undoubtedly opened my eyes. Perhaps you can use your gift to soften his heart."

Relieved, Carmen got up and left the church with the minister. She shook his hand again, thanked him and headed home.

On Carmen's street, a boy sat on the sidewalk next to his scooter holding a broken wheel. Carmen knelt beside him and said, "Wow, you must be an awesome rider. This scooter can't even handle you." She took the wheel, tapped it against the bent axle and, using her magic, snapped it all back into place.

"Hey, thanks, lady." The boy got up and scooted down the sidewalk.

Then another boy who had stolen a girl's skipping rope suffered Carmen's wrath when she tied his shoelaces together and caused him to fall onto the grass. Carmen picked up the skipping rope and said, "You get served what you deserve."

She handed the rope to the girl. "Everything is going to be okay." She directed the comment to herself, too.

Peter sat at his desk in front of his computer and typed "telekinesis" into Google. He needed to find answers and gain an understanding of what Carmen had demonstrated.

Shelley moped around the house, running to the door and from room to room, and then she laid her head on Peter's feet, whimpering. "I know, girl. You miss Carmen too."

He also searched "psychokinesis" and learned that it derived from the Greek for "mind movement." It involved moving objects and levitation using the mind. The website referred to psychokinesis as the ability of a person to influence a physical system without physical contact.

He noted that there was no scientific evidence that it was a real phenomenon, but he persisted because this resembled the control that Carmen had.

Peter jotted notes about controlling and manipulating objects.

Perhaps he could learn to understand this. Maybe it wasn't so strange and rare. He still loved Carmen, especially since the initial shock had worn off. He wondered if he could talk to his mother about this.

Carmen changed into her tiger-print pajamas, poured herself a cup of green tea and sat down in her armchair, turning on the evening news.

The top story tonight was about a child molester, who had committed a heinous crime with multiple victims. Police had found four bodies. Two more children were still missing, and their parents were begging for their children's safe return.

Carmen felt sick for the parents. She wished them calmness. She felt helpless, as her powers couldn't reach the children if she didn't see them or know where they were.

The courtroom video of the offender, Derek Moore, showed a remorseless man smirking. The reporter said he had refused to disclose the location of the other children and, of course, refused to admit that there even were any other children.

What a creepy-looking man, Carmen thought. *His eyes are evil.* She leaned forward to get a better look. "Oh my goodness!" As the guards walked him away in handcuffs and ankle shackles, the felon had the gall to wink at the camera. *He is the driver of the green minivan that was in the area when that boy Brandon Harrison went missing.*

A shiver ran through Carmen. She rubbed her arms and noticed that she had goosebumps. *Why is it that criminals get away with torture, but the police won't use it to find out where these children are? Or do they?*

Well, I'm not under the rules of the police. "Derek

Moore, I scourge you with blindness until you tell the police where the children are. I cast a haze over your eyes so all can see." *And I'll send a letter to the police to tell you what I have done to you and why. Maybe then we'll get results. There is always a day of reckoning.*

She began writing the note, and she planned to send a copy to the newspaper, anonymously, of course, when it was completed.

When she finished her tea, she put the cup in the sink and headed to bed.

She decided that she would phone Peter when she figured that he had had enough time to hear about the child molester and the letter, and perhaps then he would understand what it was that she did.

The next day, before the day became too hot, Carmen ventured through her backyard assessing the condition of her gardens. Plants had grown taller quickly, but unfortunately, so had the weeds. However, it wouldn't take her long to get things tidy again.

The peonies were just opening up and revealing their delicate fragrance. She gently held a large bloom in her hand and brought her face down to inhale the beautiful scent. Her grandmother had loved peonies, and this particular plant had come from her garden. The vibrant dark pink had been Carmen's favourite, so her grandmother had split the plant and given half of it to her. She had planted it right here beside the patio so that she felt as though her grandmother was sitting beside her. Now, with her grandmother gone, that was more important than ever.

The bleeding hearts, her favourites, were also blooming, but they were so fragile. The weak stems broke easily in the wind or under the weight of a curious squirrel. Carmen had felt fragile the last few days too. She felt like her heart was bleeding as she waited for Peter to call.

A dandelion grew beside the bleeding heart, reminding Carmen of her mother waiting to overtake her. She snapped the flowers off the weed and then pulled out the long, straight root. The white milky fluid oozed out of the broken plant. *You are no longer my weed, Mother. You say you want a better relationship with me, then let's see some proof in the pudding.*

She decided to work in her garden that morning and then go to see her mother after lunch. Although she worked at the hospital, she would comply with the visiting hours. She knew how hard it was to work with visitors asking questions or getting in the way.

Gardening was good therapy for Carmen. She knelt in the grass and gently raked the weeds out with the little garden fork. She listened to the birds singing and chirping and fighting. Carmen realized that the bird feeders were almost empty. That must have been what made them fight.

She was pleased when she saw the gentler birds— the sparrows, the finches, the doves, the starlings—getting along. The blue jays were noisy and pushy. They and the grackles were too big for the bird feeders and caused them to sway; however, the doves foraged under the feeders for the seeds that fell off. The chipmunks scavenged through the grass for the spillage as well, but only after their dish of sunflower seeds and peanuts had been exhausted.

When Carmen's bag was full of garden waste, she put her tools away and headed back into the house. She washed up and then made a salmon sandwich with fresh dill from her garden. She placed some pickles and a sliced apple on the side of the plate and returned outside with her meal. She sat beside the peony bush to eat her lunch, but the peonies weren't very good company. She yearned for Peter. *Forget it*, she thought. *I should call Diana. She isn't working today either. Maybe she wants to go out for dinner.*

Carmen went inside, put her dishes in the sink and picked up the phone.

Diana agreed to meet for dinner.

"How about we go to the little Chinese restaurant on River Street? I haven't eaten there for quite a while." Carmen chose it because she had never been there with Peter. The fewer things there were to remind her of him, the better.

"Sure. I've wanted to try that place," Diana said.

"I just have to go see my mom in the hospital first, okay?" Carmen said.

"Oh, how is she doing?" Diana asked.

"Probably better than the car that hit her." Carmen chuckled.

"I know. She is one tough cookie."

"That's for sure. Worst patient ever." Carmen laughed again.

"I'll meet you at the restaurant at five, then," Diana said.

Carmen was a little unsure about going to see her mother. Would she be her old self? It was rather hard to change almost sixty years of grouchy. But it was the right thing to do.

She had been transferred from the ICU to the rehab floor, and of course, she was grumbling. *She is never going to change*, thought Carmen.

"What's the matter, Mom?" Carmen said without the traditional greeting. "Is this not the five-star hotel that you had hoped it would be?" She pulled a chair from the corner and sat beside her mother's wheelchair.

"No, it's not, and don't be a smart-ass," Norma snapped. "The food sucks and the place smells and the nurses walk away from me when I'm talking."

"Gee, I can't imagine why." Carmen snickered.

"There you go being a smart-ass again."

"Mom, please just concentrate on getting better, and be nice to the nurses and other patients. Then things will go much smoother." Carmen tidied the meal table and noticed flowers on the side table. "Who are those from?" She found the card within the flowers and pulled it out. "Hey, they're from Jill. How sweet." Carmen smiled and waved the card toward her mother.

"Showing up in person would have been sweet. This is just the easy way out," Norma growled. She pulled a face while repositioning herself in her chair. "Carmen, help me get into bed, will you? I'm tired."

Carmen helped her lie down for a nap and then

excused herself. She said hello as she passed the nurses' station and then headed outside.

Relieved to be away from the negativity, she raised her face to the sun and took in a deep breath.

It wasn't time to meet Diana yet, so she went home and did some organizing. It was amazing how the papers piled up. No sooner had she filed and shredded, then more papers came in the mail or from work.

When her basket of papers was empty, she went upstairs, fixed herself up and headed to River Street. She had put on white denim capris and a sleeveless purple-and-white polka dot blouse that cinched in at the waist and flared at the hips. Her lavender sandals with the one-inch heels topped off the outfit.

Diana arrived after Carmen, wearing a bright-orange dress with large red flowers in the print. It flattered her strawberry-blonde hair. "Hi, Carmen. You look great. It's nice to see you with your clothes on." She laughed.

"Watch it. You're just adding to the gossip." Carmen laughed too.

"But we aren't at work. Besides, who cares if you and Peter are seeing each other? Yours certainly isn't the first hospital romance. Rob and Gayle were dating before they got married. Betty just wants something to gossip about, and your story was the best one she could find."

"Well, we aren't seeing each other anymore. Plus, Betty doesn't like me."

"That's only because she's jealous. Everyone else likes you."

"You look awesome in that dress," Carmen said. "If

you were to add a hat, you would spark the memory of our dear late Princess Diana."

They chose a table by the far window with oleander bushes on either side. "I love these," Diana said, touching the delicate pink flowers. "But mine always got mealy bugs. The plants I have now are the kind that *no one* could kill." She picked up the menu.

"Gee, it's good you aren't that way with your patients," Carmen teased.

While they were eating, Carmen noticed that a woman at a table nearby had left part of her salad, part of the roll and part of her entrée on her plates. She refused a doggy bag and told the waiter that she never ate leftovers.

You have obviously never gone hungry, Carmen thought.

Carmen saw to it that all the food in the fridge at the woman's home was now spoiled. *I know you can replace it easily enough, but this might just make you think.*

The two coworkers had a pleasant dinner, laughing frequently, which helped Carmen to forget her troubles.

Carmen took her doggy bag of shrimp scampi, hugged Diana and headed home.

I have no problem with eating leftovers, Carmen reflected. *It means I don't have to cook tomorrow night either.* She put the pasta in the fridge and imagined the woman coming home to the rotten food. *She will be checking expiry dates and the plug on the fridge. She will be stumped.*

As Carmen folded laundry, someone knocked on the door.

Carmen peeked through the glass in the front door

before opening it. She was surprised to see Sergeant Campbell. He had a shoebox in his hands that made Carmen quite excited. *Could it be?*

She had been worried that she wouldn't care about the jewellery anymore. At one point, she didn't care if she ever got it back because she felt her grandmother had betrayed her. But now that it might be here, she knew she would be happy to have it again.

When she found out about the theft, Jill had offered to split her half of the inheritance with Carmen, but Carmen would have nothing to do with that. However, she was thrilled to get her things back. She knew she still loved her grandmother and realized that she must have had a good reason for keeping the secret. Her grandfather had probably insisted on keeping it quiet.

"Come in, Sergeant Campbell." She held the door for him and waved him in.

"Thank ye, lassie. You have a lovely home." He handed her the box. "I rushed the processing of the evidence for you so you could get your things back. The other things will have to wait a bit longer, though."

"Thank you so much. I appreciate that very sincerely," Carmen said. She opened the box and felt choked up. She looked inside. It seemed like everything was there, all of the jewellery that she remembered her grandmother wearing that Carmen and Jill had divided. She pulled one item out of the box. "This isn't part of my grandmother's collection." She held it up for the Sergeant to see.

"That was in the bag that Roberts brought to the pawn shop. I thought it was yours. Are you sure it isn't?"

He scratched his head. "I guess I need to take it back and look for the rightful owner." He took it from her, tipped his hat and turned back to the door.

"Thank you again, Sergeant Campbell," Carmen said as she followed him out onto the front porch. She went back inside and sat down with the box of jewellery. "I'm sorry I ever doubted you, Grandma. I still love you." She tightly clenched a pendant and held it to her chest.

14

Sergeant Campbell returned to the police station with the extra piece of jewellery. He looked at it, wondering where it might have come from. Was it misplaced here, or had Roberts brought it to the pawnshop? Perhaps the pawnshop owner had included it by mistake. He would go to the shop and ask the clerk. Meanwhile, he would look through the long list of descriptions of other lost items.

He was unable to match it with any other pieces reported stolen. He placed it in his desk drawer.

"Mrs. Roberts, do you happen to be missing any jewellery?" Sergeant Campbell asked when he called. "I have something here that was given to me by the pawnshop owner that doesn't belong to Carmen Hamilton."

"I haven't noticed anything missing, but I'll take a look." She put the phone down before the Sergeant could answer.

He waited on the other end of the line.

"No, I don't seem to be missing any jewellery," Mrs.

Roberts said a couple minutes later. "Why, what does it look like?"

"Thank you for checking, Mrs. Roberts. Have a nice evening." He quickly hung up so she couldn't ask any more questions. *Tomorrow I will return to the pawnshop.*

Campbell tediously sifted through evidence lists from throughout Ontario on the computer system, searching for something similar to the necklace from Carmen. Finally he found a match: an 18-inch chain with a dolphin pendant made of 24-karat gold with a 0.1-carat diamond chip for an eye. It was linked to a woman from Montreal, Gabriella Babineaux. She had been reported missing back in 2007. Her body had been found nine months later in the Green Briar Meadows of Sherbrooke, Quebec.

She was dead. Now he certainly had to return to the pawnshop.

The night was still young and Carmen had dinner calories to burn off, so she went for a walk. She had heard about a car show at the local burger joint, so she headed there.

She weaved between the cars, looking them over and peeking inside, chatting with the owners. They sure had a passion for their cars.

A man who was also looking at the cars followed Carmen, looking at the cars and then at her. He got close and peeked into a car. Carmen walked to the next car. The man followed casually, still watching her.

"Not too many women are interested in cars," he said.

She looked at him and continued her viewing.

"I mean, most wouldn't come to look at cars without a guy dragging them along. So I'm guessing you're single." He smiled at her. He had long, dark-blond hair and a goatee, and he wore a jean jacket with the sleeves cut off. He was not her type at all.

"Sorry, I'm not looking for anything right now," Carmen assured the greasy man.

"Hey, no strings, just a good time. Then you never have to look at me again if you don't want." He threw his head back to swish his hair.

Oh, please! Carmen thought. *How creepy can you get?* "No thanks. I just had a bad breakup and don't want anything right now."

"Oh, man, that's too bad. He was nuts to let *you* go."

"He dumped *me.*"

"What? The guy must be crazy, 'cause you're hot."

Carmen chuckled a little. "Gee, your approach really needs some work."

"Hey, that's not very nice. I just gave you a compliment. You think you're too good for me, don't you?"

"No, you're trying to get me into bed. Now, if you don't mind, I'd like to have some space." Carmen walked away quickly, squeezing past a crowd of people that would separate her from the man.

A skanky-looking woman owned the next car on display. She came out and leaned against the fender. The distasteful man rushed over to her. *Now she is more your type*, she thought. The man looked at Carmen and turned up his nose. *Oh, really, like I would care.* She giggled.

I'm sure you don't eat broccoli, but let's stick a little bit between your teeth, just for effect. Carmen laughed. A man beside a blue convertible looked at Carmen and asked her what was so funny.

"Whoso diggeth a pit shall fall therein," she quoted from Proverbs with a smile.

The man looked down at the ground, probably expecting to see a hole.

Carmen continued looking at the cars and witnessed a little boy pick some flowering weeds for his mommy. He handed them to her, and she patted his head. "Thank you, darling."

Carmen quickly produced a shiny blue balloon and offered it to the boy. His face lit up, and he looked to his mom for permission to accept it. "Yes, you may have the balloon," she said. He reached for it, grinning from ear to ear.

Carmen tied the paper ribbon loosely to his wrist to keep it from floating away.

"Thank you," his mother said to Carmen. Then she reached for the little boy's hand and led him to the candy-apple red pickup truck. The boy turned and looked at Carmen. "She's magic, Mommy."

His mother answered in a conciliatory manner, "Yes, dear."

15

Peering over a pile of towels, washcloths and a hospital gown, Carmen prepared the bedside table for the washbasin. She moved things aside and greeted the elderly man in the bed. "Good morning. I am Carmen, your nurse. I'm here to give you your sponge bath."

"Good morning," he replied, sitting up a little straighter.

Carmen pulled the curtain around the bed and took the basin to fill it with hot water. She came back to his bedside and helped him remove his hospital gown. Then she lathered a washcloth and started washing him while he talked.

The patient told Carmen all about his life experiences from his full-time career in the military. "I was a pilot in World War II. I flew hundreds of missions into enemy territory. I lost my leg in a parachuting accident and then they grounded me. I have three medals and a great pension."

"That sounds exciting," Carmen said as she rinsed the cloth in the basin.

"I've been to Hawaii, Fiji, Germany, Japan, Thailand, New Zealand and other exciting countries."

Carmen imagined these places and envisioned the experiences of skydiving, skiing and scuba diving. She helped him to roll over and washed his back. She dried him and applied lotion.

"I never got married but had many friends. I also have five brothers, and they all have wives and children, and they invite me to all the family functions. I lived in a condo, and came and went as I pleased. I just recently went into a nursing home. They cook for me, and do my laundry. I don't have to lift a finger."

Carmen imagined her life alone. Would she do all those adventurous things? She would like to, but instead she pictured herself going to work and coming home to an empty house, day after day. "You've had a busy life," Carmen said as she straightened the bed sheets. She took the basin and towels and walked into the bathroom.

When she came back, he said to her, "You are an angel."

"Thanks. People say that to us all the time."

"I know, but you really are. You're different; I can feel it. When you touch me, I feel the energy. You have the power of healing, don't you?"

Carmen was more interested now. She came closer to him. "I do, a little bit, but it isn't strong enough to heal serious matters." *What am I doing? I should never tell people that.* She stifled her next utterance.

"Touch me again." He reached for her hand. "See? I *do* feel it. I want to die. I'm tired and in pain, and I have lived a full life."

"That is not up to me, George. I will do everything I can to keep you alive and comfortable, but the rest is between you and God. I cannot change your destiny. I can't even plot my own life."

"But you're an angel. You could ask him to take me."

"No, George, I'm not able to do that anymore than you could, except through prayer. All I can give you is comfort and peace." She touched his forehead. He closed his eyes, and an expression of serenity came to his face.

"Me, too," the man in the next bed said, sitting upright quickly. "Touch me too!"

She walked around the curtain separating the two beds and touched his shoulder. She closed her eyes, felt his pain and wished it away.

"What are you doing with my patient?" Tina bellowed as she walked into the room.

"It worked! It worked!" the patient hollered. "The pain is gone. Thank you."

Carmen looked up, walked slowly to Tina and leaned to her ear. "Something that you are incapable of."

The first floor of the hospital contained the Diagnostic Imaging Department, which housed the X-ray, ultrasound and MRI machines. This was very expensive equipment, and Peter and Rob were here to do the routine monthly maintenance. This was not a good time for Peter to be out of sorts. He had been off his game for the four days now since he had rejected Carmen's confession.

He had talked to Rob about it already and had played it over in his mind again and again. He tried to forget her at first but then thought that he could possibly accept her for who she was, and even her oddities. However, he always came back to fear of what she might be capable of, especially if she felt the need to punish him.

He juggled the idea of never telling her about his past, but he knew that was not part of a healthy marriage. Yes, he had considered asking her to marry him. Perhaps it was lucky that she had told him about herself before he had done that.

It was hard to get advice from Rob without giving him the whole story. Rob would never believe it. So, of course, Rob told Peter that there couldn't be anything so bad about her that would warrant his dropping her and walking away.

"Peter, wake up. Snap out of it, man. You're going to mess up big time if you don't get on the ball, and you look like shit too, you know. You haven't shaved, you've got bags under your eyes and you walk like an orangutan. If this is so hard, why don't you crawl to her door and beg her to take you back? Have you taken a good look at the girl? Man, she is gorgeous, smart and nice, and she makes good money and likes *you*. That in itself is the clincher. I mean, who else would put up with you?" He laughed and shoved Peter's shoulder.

"You put up with me," Peter retorted.

"I get paid to put up with you." Rob laughed. "No, really, you are falling apart. What could be wrong with her? Was she a man before? Because really, that is about all that would count for giving her the heave-ho." Peter didn't answer, so Rob tried again. "In jail, an abortion, has six kids, picks her nose, what?"

"Stop it." Peter packed up his tools and pulled out the clipboard to start the paperwork. "You wouldn't believe me anyway."

"What are you talking about? Is she Cat Woman?"

"Something like that."

"You're full of crap, man." He paused and then punched Peter's arm. "Because Cat Woman is hot as hell." He laughed. "Come on, I give up. Let's go for lunch."

Back on the fourth floor, Carmen was trying to console Diana. "I go through all that work cleaning the fridge, and you were the only person who said anything. Sometimes I feel like I'm invisible. People cut me off or walk away when I talk. And with some of the cliques around here, I feel like I don't fit in." She put her hands on her hips.

"You did a great job with the fridge, Diana. I am sure people noticed, they just don't bother to say anything. It's sad. And it isn't just you. I get cut off sometimes too. It's the same people doing it all the time, and they don't even realize it. Come on, let's go sit outside for lunch."

At the door to the patio, Diana headed out first but then turned abruptly and pushed Carmen back into the building. "Peter's there. Do you still want to go?"

"Not!" Carmen turned abruptly and headed back down the hallway.

They reached the next door to the inner hallway and stopped. "This sucks," Carmen said. "Why is this happening? I try so hard to be a decent person, and all I get is kicked in the ass. I'm thirty-five, have waited so long for someone, and now that I find him, he is ripped away from me." She sobbed and leaned against the door. "Part of me wants to run out there and shake him."

Diana put her hand on Carmen's shoulder. "You are a good person, and I truly believe that you will get what you are due."

Carmen looked away. "Maybe I already have."

That evening, Carmen sat in her favourite chair with a bowl of grapes listening to the news while she did a crossword puzzle since half the news' visuals bored her. Peter had teased her about doing the puzzles in pen. He asked if she was overly confident or just super smart. "I just plan ahead before I fill in the word," she had said. There she went again, thinking about him. Carmen pushed his image from her mind. It was just too painful.

Seven-letter word for grief; *starts with an* A. *Hmm. Anguish. No problem getting that word.* "Stop feeling sorry for yourself, woman!"

She put her crossword puzzle down on her lap when she heard the topic of the next story: "Accused child molester Derek Moore still refuses to tell police the whereabouts of the two missing children. He denies his involvement. Families of the children are panic stricken, worrying about their children.

"The mother of missing seven-year-old boy Brandon Harrison was permitted by police to face Moore and begged him to return her child. Moore barely flinched, stating that he did not even know who the boy was. The woman needed sedation after the meeting."

The anchor turned to a different camera. "No further contact from the letter writer, yet Moore remains blind. Police are at a loss."

The newscast angered her. "This is ridiculous. Enough already." Determined to bring this man to a confession, she decided to add insult to injury and paralyzed Moore on his left side. She began writing another letter:

> Derek Moore, this letter comes to you as you find yourself paralyzed on your left side. Apparently, blindness was not enough for you. I will restore your vision only long enough to read this letter, as I want you to believe that this is indeed directed to you from me. You will unveil the location of the children upon receiving this letter or you will find the right side of your body paralyzed as well. Justice will be served.

Carmen knew that she had no time to lose, so she went directly to the police station. She approached a teenage boy walking past. "Hey, how would you like to earn twenty bucks?"

Looking warily at Carmen, he asked, "How?"

"Go inside and deliver this letter personally." She pointed to the police station.

"What's in the envelope?"

"A letter. You can help find some missing kids." She waved the twenty-dollar bill in front of him.

"Are you the one who has the kids?"

"No. Look, kid, there's no time to waste." Carmen pushed the letter at him. "Just give this letter to a cop, okay?"

He took the letter and the bill.

She walked away quickly, checking from a distance that he went inside.

On her way home, she imagined the police in a frenzy interrogating the boy about who gave him the letter.

Later, the news described Carmen as a witch, an angel, magical and supernatural. They requested that she come to the police station and reveal herself.

"Do they think I'm crazy?" She knew that this was out of the question, for she would become iconic and would never have peace.

Nevertheless, Carmen's demands were successful, and Moore confessed. "I'll tell you where the children are, just keep that crazy woman away from me. There is an old shed behind an abandoned farmhouse on Rural Road Six. I have it locked up with a chain and padlock. Brandon Harrison is one of the kids. Now tell that crazy bitch to give me my sight back."

The newscaster later disclosed that a squad of police officers had raced to the address, found the shed and cut the padlock. Inside the dark, dingy shed were two dirty, frightened and dehydrated children huddled in a corner.

They showed the parents of the children on the screen, and they were ecstatic.

Carmen was thrilled for them. She blessed them all with serenity. The children had been sent to the hospital where Carmen worked. She hoped she could get a look at them at some point.

Before she went to bed, she returned Moore's eyesight and the use of his left side. However, she took away his libido. "They are burnt, like moths in a flame," she muttered while crawling under the sheets.

Peter had been following the news too and speculated that Carmen might have intervened. When the boy was interviewed, he described the woman who had asked him to deliver the letter to the police department, and then he was sure. At first, his fear still clouded his mind. But then his curiosity got the best of him, his fear diminished and he remembered how much he loved her.

He felt surprisingly proud, and then he intensely missed her and thought that maybe she wasn't so scary after all. *She is incredible*, he realized. *She does use this power for good, just like she said. I was mean to judge her. I have to make things right.*

As Carmen pulled into her driveway after picking up some groceries, she noticed a police cruiser parked on the street. Her powers put her on full alert. "Damn," she whispered as she saw Sergeant Campbell get out of the car. "They know. Damn it! They know!"

"Hi, Sergeant," Carmen said as she got out of the car, trying to hide her panic. "Did you find out where that other necklace came from?"

"Can I take your groceries for you?" he asked, reaching for her bag. She accepted his offer. "No, I haven't yet. I am narrowing it down, though."

"Thank you. What brings you here this time?"

"I wanted to ask if you knew anything about the letter sent to Derek Moore."

Carmen almost choked on her own saliva. "Only what I have heard on the news," she stuttered.

"The description of the woman who delivered it to the police sounds a lot like you." Sergeant Campbell squinted.

"What? Do you mean the woman who claims to have blinded Derek Moore? How do they even know what she looks like?" Carmen took a breath to calm herself.

"The boy who delivered the letter gave us a description. It sounds a lot like you." He walked to the house with her.

"I am not that woman," Carmen lied. "I don't mean to rush you, but I need to put these things away. I have another engagement. I'm sorry." She took the bag of groceries back and unlocked the front door.

"Good day, Miss Hamilton." The Sergeant tipped his

hat and dropped the subject, but he turned and gave her a suspicious look when he reached his car.

Carmen went inside and set the groceries on the kitchen counter. "Damn," she said again.

The phone rang. It was her mother. She felt desperate enough that even talking to her mother would help. "Hi, Mom."

"Nice job," Norma said.

"Pardon?"

"Nice job blinding the kidnapper. Your little trick helped."

"Thanks, I guess. I was determined. That creep had to disclose where the kids were before they died of dehydration. Now he will never get out of prison."

"You don't have to justify it to me. I agree with you. I wish I had the guts to use my powers."

"How did you know it was me?" Carmen put the carton of milk in the fridge.

"They described you on the news. I just figured it out."

The next day, although exhausted, Carmen headed off to work. *This power can be draining*, she thought, *but I still have to make a living*. Carmen always felt tired or weak after she manipulated the world around her, and the effect intensified as she got older and her powers became stronger.

The more passionate she felt about something, the more strength her powers had. When she felt loved, as she only realized recently when she had been with Peter, she was stronger than ever. Her powers held better focus; they were more intense. But without him, she felt clumsy and awkward and had to struggle to maintain control.

She realized then that he had been a key to her completeness. She needed him. She needed to convince him to accept her. They were soul mates. Only he wouldn't answer her phone calls. *What should I do?*

While standing at the cross walk waiting for the signal to change, a loud noise startled her. Plywood boards had slid out of the back of an SUV. Tires screeched behind the truck, and the driver slammed on the brakes. *Why didn't I notice that happening? I could have prevented that. I am losing my intuition.*

Two construction workers ran over and lifted the boards back onto the truck. The driver shook their hands and thanked them. They brushed it off as the right thing to do.

Carmen was pleased, so she thought for a moment before granting them their reward. They would realize once they took their hardhats off that they had full heads of lush hair again. *Do good and good will come to you*, she thought.

The walk signal engaged and traffic moved again. Carmen continued on her way to work. *I hope there will be a domino effect today.* It seemed that when people saw others helping, they felt so inclined to do the same. The Black Eyed Peas said it best: "This is the effect, the domino effect."

Reaching her floor, she noticed that all the staff was at the nurses' station, including the manager, who informed them. "Tina has been admitted to the ICU. She has had a CVA. She is stable but in need of monitoring. Doctors managed to treat her in time for the clot-busting procedure, but they are uncertain about the extent of the damage. We will keep you informed. Please pray for her, and if anyone feels the need for counselling, please see me in my office."

People gasped and the chatter began, but a patient who asked for help distracted Carmen, and she was grateful to be excused. The day went on with babble about Tina, and Carmen actually got tired of it and wished the girls would get their work done.

No one wanted to say that Tina deserved what she got, but Carmen knew that would be the consensus. People could be so phony during a crisis. They had always talked badly about Tina, but now, everyone seemed so concerned. Of course, no one wished a stroke on anyone, but there was no need to be hypocritical.

A few of the girls went to see Tina and reported that she was awake and out of danger. She would probably have no deficits from the stroke since they had caught it in time. She would be transferred soon to a medical bed.

One of the nurses joked about what a lousy patient Tina would be and felt sorry for the nurses that would be taking care of her. They would most likely not admit Tina to the floor that she worked on.

16

On the route home from Rachel's eye doctor appointment, the conversation of the case of Derek Moore became the topic. Peter was driving Rachel home because the eye doctor had dilated her pupils. She sat in the passenger seat with the visor down and her sunglasses on, still squinting from the bright sunshine.

"That entire case was strange, beginning with the blindness, then the anonymous letter and then the paralysis," Rachel said. "But it worked. The threat to paralyze him entirely was just enough to make him squeal like the pig he is. But how did the writer of the letter blind him and then paralyze him? Is there a drug that could do that? Could it have been a guard or the police?"

The questions were rhetorical, but Peter wanted to confide in his mother so much that he was ready to burst. He wanted to tell her about Carmen and ask her opinion. Was she right that he was protecting Carmen's privacy because he still wanted her in his future? If he was now so eager to tell her the truth, did it mean that he no longer wanted Carmen in his future? No, he wanted Carmen so much it hurt. He had missed her so much that he could face any punishment from her.

"Mom, do you remember that I told you there was something weird about Carmen, a secret?" He didn't wait for her answer, but he knew that she nodded. "I didn't want to tell you about it then, but I do now. I need you to keep this a secret." Peter looked straight ahead as he drove. Saying this would be so much easier without having to look at her.

"Certainly, dear. I can keep any secret you ask me to keep." Rachel repositioned the visor and her glasses.

Peter drove down a long road lined with overhanging trees that created a tunnel of leaves. Peter knew that his mother loved this road, and the shade of the trees would give her sensitive eyes relief.

"Carmen is the one who wrote that letter." He hesitated to wait for his mother's reaction.

"Pardon?"

He repeated himself more slowly this time so that she could take it in. "Carmen is also the one who blinded Moore and paralyzed him. Now, don't think of her as cruel, because she does this only to people who deserve it."

"What are you talking about? How could someone do that?"

"Because he deserved it, and it was an excellent strategy to get him to reveal where the other children were, as you heard. It worked just as Carmen planned." Peter gripped the steering wheel tightly at ten and two, waiting for her response.

"No, I mean, how does somebody make someone else blind? She was nowhere near the police station when he went blind. And she wasn't at the hospital when he became paralyzed." She reached over and grabbed Peter's arm. "Or was she? She works at the hospital!"

"No, Mom, it's not like that. She has … here we go … special powers." He swallowed hard. He couldn't believe what he was saying.

Rachel laughed. "Special powers? Like Batman, taking revenge on the men who killed his parents? No, wait, Cat Woman."

"Mom, this isn't funny. She isn't Cat Woman. She's more, telekinetic, or something like that. She was born that way, and I have seen her use her ability."

"Really, you've seen this? This was the secret you were keeping? Why did you break up over something like this?"

They reached Rachel's house but sat in the driveway for a while.

"I was worried that she would use her skill on me and punish me." He wrung his hands in his lap. He looked down.

"What could you possibly need punishment for?" Peter's mother touched his shoulder. "You are a wonderful man, and I am more proud of you than words could ever express." She raised her hand to stroke his cheek. "Plus, you know I love you more than anything."

"Mom, when I was eighteen, I had an affair with an older, married teacher. Her husband found out and their marriage fell apart, and she lost her job. She broke down, he proved her unfit and so he got custody of their daughter and she was devastated. It was only a fling, but I was too weak to resist her advances."

He cradled the steering wheel with his arms and leaned his forehead on them. "I have kept this to myself all these years. I am ashamed of myself, but recently I thought it would be something that Carmen should know, because I bought a ring for her. I wanted to be honest right from the start. But then I was scared that she would use her powers to punish me somehow for what I did."

Rachel put her hand on Peter's leg. "Peter, you were eighteen, full of hormones and confusion. The teacher should have known better; she was the older one. Why did you torment yourself with this for so long? Carmen will not punish you for this. You have done that enough to yourself. Go to her, Peter. Give her that ring." She leaned over, kissed him and got out of the car. "Thanks for the ride. See, you are a good man."

Having returned to the roof of the bank, Carmen felt as if she had come full circle but no further ahead. She felt sad and lonely, and the more she thought about it, the more angry she felt. Life had dealt her a lousy hand, and it sucked.

"Well, Ralph, do you think this is my destiny, to sit here with you, the man in my life made of stone? Is this all there is? Or, should I alter who I am and give up my powers?" Carmen rose above the ledge that she was sitting on, did a backwards roll in the air and came back down to sit beside Ralph, putting her arm around the ugly, cold gargoyle. "I guess it is just you and me, because this is who I am, and I like my powers. The only thing better would be if Peter liked them too."

From where she sat, Carmen could see the old woman with the many bird feeders on her porch. She filled them every day without fail. Birds faithfully flitted to her, splashing in the birdbath and making the old woman laugh. Chickadees sat on her hand to eat, having become tame from the woman's kindness. This already was the woman's reward. Nonetheless, Carmen had granted her with a special blessing years before. The woman was now one hundred and three years old.

To the right, Carmen had a perfect view of the skateboard park. The floodlights allowed her to see three boys still skating up and down the ramps.

The smallest boy fell and sat holding his knee. Even with the kneepads on, he had managed to hurt himself. The taller boy came over, inspected the knee and helped the injured boy back to his feet. The other boy carried the skateboards as they headed away.

Carmen granted that when the little one got home, there would be no sign of injury to his knee.

Carmen felt satisfied with her gift, so she leaned back onto Ralph. She looked up at the stars and watched the bats fly back and forth chasing bugs.

And, when she looked back down at her town, illuminated by the street lights, she could see the figure of the man that she loved walking up the path to the front door of her home.

Printed in the United States
By Bookmasters